P9-CEH-426

Whatever After

SPILL the BEANS

Read all the Whatever After books!

#1: Fairest of All

#2: If the Shoe Fits

#3: Sink or Swim

#4: Dream On

#5: Bad Hair Day

#6: Cold as Ice

#7: Beauty Queen

#8: Once Upon a Frog

#9: Genie in a Bottle

#10: Sugar and Spice

#11: Two Peas in a Pod

#12: Seeing Red

#13: Spill the Beans

Special Edition #1:

Abby in Wonderland

Whatever After

SPILL the BEANS

SARAH MLYNOWSKI

 Scholastic Press/New York

Copyright © 2019 by Sarah Mlynowski

All rights reserved. Published by Scholastic Press, an imprint of Scholastic Inc., *Publishers since 1920.* SCHOLASTIC, SCHOLASTIC PRESS, and associated logos are trademarks and/or registered trademarks of Scholastic Inc.

The publisher does not have any control over and does not assume any responsibility for author or third-party websites or their content.

No part of this publication may be reproduced, stored in a retrieval system, or transmitted in any form or by any means, electronic, mechanical, photocopying, recording, or otherwise, without written permission of the publisher. For information regarding permission, write to Scholastic Inc., Attention: Permissions Department, 557 Broadway, New York, NY 10012.

This book is a work of fiction. Names, characters, places, and incidents are either the product of the author's imagination or are used fictitiously, and any resemblance to actual persons, living or dead, business establishments, events, or locales is entirely coincidental.

Library of Congress Cataloging-in-Publication Data available

ISBN 978-1-338-16297-4

10 9 8 7 6 5 4 3 2 1   19 20 21 22 23

Printed in the U.S.A.   23

First edition, May 2019

for beaux and edan rozin

chapter one

Face-plant

You know when something is bothering you and you can't stop thinking about it?

Welcome to my life.

Right now, I'm sitting on the bleachers with my mom, watching my little brother's soccer game. Is the game distracting me from my troubles? It is not.

The Smithville Scooters (that's Jonah's team) are playing the Fryton Academy Wildcats. And even though it's sunny and breezy and my mom just bought me a pink lemonade punch from the snack bar, I can't stop thinking about what happened at school earlier today. It's like a mosquito bite that won't stop itching me.

I sigh and slump in my seat. I take another sip of my pink lemonade.

My mom turns to me. "Are you okay, Abby? You seem kind of mopey."

"Frankie and Robin got into an argument," I explain. Frankie and Robin are my two best friends. "And they want me to pick sides."

My mom frowns. "That sounds tricky," she says. "Want to tell me what happened?"

On the field, the soccer players are chasing the ball. I see Jonah running with his teammates, and I hope he won't mind that I'm barely paying attention to what he's doing out there.

"Well," I tell my mom, "Frankie was invited to Daria's birthday party on Saturday night. Daria is new and she doesn't know that many people, so Frankie said she'd go."

"That's nice of Frankie," Mom says. She peers out at the field to check on Jonah, then looks back at me. "So what's the problem?"

I sigh again. "Frankie already had plans with Robin and me for Saturday night. FRAM night."

FRA stands for *Frankie*, *Robin*, and *Abby* (the *M* stands for *Movie*). The three of us even used to have matching necklaces that said *FRA*. But then Penny joined our group — she's Robin's other best friend. And then we became FRAP.

We started movie night two weeks ago, but so far it's just been me, Frankie, and Robin who can make it. Penny is always busy on Saturday nights. She has all these events to attend with her parents. Like weddings. Or a sweet sixteen. "We're a very popular family," Penny told us, with a flick of her blond ponytail. Which is totally fine by me. I'm thrilled that movie night can be the original three. FRA for the win!

"And you're upset that Frankie can't come this time?" Mom prods me.

I nod. "Yeah, but I'm not as upset as Robin is. She got really mad at Frankie."

I cringe at the memory of my two best friends facing off as we stood together in the school hallway after the last bell.

"A birthday party is only ONCE a year," Frankie had said to a frowning Robin. "Movie night is EVERY Saturday. So it's not a big deal if I miss it."

But Frankie missing movie night IS a big deal. We take turns hosting. I hosted the first week (because it was my idea), then last weekend was Frankie's turn, and now it's Robin's. The host gets to pick the movie, too. We make a huge bowl of popcorn, and in another bowl, we mix together at least five different kinds of candy. Swedish Fish. Skittles. M&M's. Milk Duds. Junior Mints. YUM. Plus, we always have a pitcher of fruit punch. I LOVE movie night.

Frankie pushed her red glasses up on her nose and turned to me. "Tell Robin I'm right."

Robin tossed her curly strawberry-blond hair behind her shoulders and also turned to me. "Tell Frankie she already has plans and should honor them and not ditch us for BETTER plans."

"They're not better plans, they're just different," Frankie argued.

I wondered why I wasn't invited to the party. Although in this case, I was glad I wasn't. Too complicated.

"Uh, I . . . Well, um . . ." I said. I took a couple of steps backward. Of course I wanted Frankie to come to our movie night. But should she turn down an invitation to a birthday party? For a new girl in school?

What was the right or wrong answer? I had no idea.

Finally, I just said, “I have to go to Jonah’s soccer game!” and raced out of the school.

“What do you think?” I ask my mom now, as we sit side by side on the bleachers. I’m hoping she’ll tell me what to do. She’s really good at giving advice. She’s a lawyer, same as my dad. He’s working on a case today, which is why he couldn’t make Jonah’s game.

“What do *you* think?” Mom asks me.

Crumbs.

I wish I knew what to think. My friends’ argument is a tough case. But I want to be a judge when I grow up, so I should be able to crack tough cases.

“I think they’re both right,” I admit.

“Then tell them that,” my mom says. “That they both have a point and then let them work it out.”

I can’t imagine that going very smoothly. I frown and sip more lemonade.

My mom suddenly turns her attention back to the field. She sits up straight and crosses her fingers. “Come on, Jonah, you can do it,” she says under her breath.

I crane my neck to see. The soccer ball has been kicked

to Jonah, who is in scoring position. I cross my fingers, too, forgetting about Frankie and Robin for the moment. My little brother looks nervous as he aims his foot at the ball and —

Oh, no!

A kid on the opposing team just kicked the ball away from Jonah! He stole the ball!

"Aww," my mother says, her shoulders falling. "Poor Jonah."

Now Jonah is trying to stop the other team from kicking the ball into the Smithville Scooters' goal. *Trying* is the key word. I cringe as my brother ends up tripping over his feet and landing face-first on the grass. And the ball goes straight into the Scooters' goal.

Double crumbs.

"GO, WILDCATS!" a lady on the bleachers shouts through a megaphone, and her side cheers like crazy.

"I hope Jonah's all right," Mom says worriedly. We watch as Jonah pushes himself up and trudges into the team huddle the coach has called. At least he's not hurt.

"I think it's an ice cream kind of night," my mom adds,

patting my knee. "Someone's going to need some cheering up."

"Oh, yeah," I say. Jonah definitely needs some cheering up. So do I.

A few minutes later, the soccer game is over. The Wildcats have won, and everyone who was rooting for Smithville is in low spirits.

Jonah comes over to me and my mom, staring at the ground. He has dirt on his cheek and all over his uniform from his face-plant. "I'm the worst soccer player ever," he tells us.

"You're a very strong player, Jonah," my mom says, giving him a hug. "And even strong players miss kicks. That's all part of the game. Winning *and* losing."

"Yeah, but I hate losing!" Jonah responds. "And everyone knows it's my fault we lost. I messed up." He looks down at the ground again, and I can see that his eyes are filled with tears.

"Let's stop and get some ice cream for dessert," Mom suggests gently, but Jonah shakes his head. When he's refusing ice cream, you know it's serious.

Suddenly, I have an idea. I know what will cheer Jonah up. And it's not ice cream.

It's a trip through our magic mirror.

You heard me right. I have a magic mirror. It's in the basement of our house. When Jonah and I knock on it three times at midnight, it takes us into a fairy tale.

If you think I'm kidding, I'm not. We've been inside twelve fairy tales already. *Cinderella. Hansel and Gretel. Little Red Riding Hood.* And those are just the highlights.

We never know which story we'll be visiting. Or why Maryrose — the fairy who is cursed to live inside our mirror — sends us there. But that's part of the fun.

Our parents don't know about the magic mirror. So Jonah and I can't visit it every single night. That would be too risky.

But we have to try tonight.

chapter two

How to Cheer Up Your Little Brother

When my alarm clock goes off a few minutes before midnight, I pop out of bed and quickly change from my pj's into a T-shirt, jeans, and a hoodie. I also put on my watch. My watch always tells us what time it is back home when we're inside a fairy tale. If it's a school night, we have to be back in Smithville by 7:00 A.M., when our parents come to wake us up.

I rush into Jonah's room. He's sprawled out on his bed, his curly brown hair sticking up all over the place. He always gets bedhead. Tonight, his mouth is turned into a frown even while he's asleep. Aww, poor Jonah.

"Hey," I say, gently shaking his shoulder. "It's mirror time. Wakey, wakey."

"What?" Jonah grumbles, opening his eyes.

"It's time to go," I say.

"Where?" he asks.

"Where do you think?" I ask. "Into a fairy tale!"

"No," he says, putting his pillow over his head. "I'm in a bad mood."

"I know!" I say. "That's why we're going. To cheer you up."

Jonah has done the same thing for me in the past. Nothing can distract you faster than a visit to a fairy tale.

And I'm still feeling down in the dumps about the Frankie-Robin fight, so I could use the distraction, too.

"*Nothing* will cheer me up," Jonah insists. "Leave me alone."

I remove the pillow from his face. "No. C'mon, it'll be great."

"It won't. I don't want to hang out with a grumpy princess right now."

"What grumpy princess?" I ask. "When do we meet grumpy princesses?"

He sits up and waves his hands over his head. "We always meet grumpy princesses! The *Princess and the Frog* princess was grumpy. And the real princess from *The Princess and the Pea* was a spoiled brat."

All right, he has a point.

"But we've met some amazing princesses," I point out. "And non-princesses. What about Little Red? I know you liked Little Red . . ."

He blushes. "I did like Little Red."

Jonah actually had a crush on Little Red! It was pretty cute, and I'm tempted to tease him about it. But I want to cheer him up now, not embarrass him.

"Maybe we'll meet someone as awesome as Little Red," I say. "Or, hey," I add, struck by an idea. "Maybe we'll meet Jack! From *Jack and the Beanstalk*!"

Jonah pouts. "We *never* get to meet Jack."

Jack and the Beanstalk is Jonah's all-time favorite fairy tale. Whenever we go through the mirror, Jonah always hopes we've landed in Jack's story. But we haven't — so far.

"Not *yet*," I say. "But maybe tonight's the night."

"You're just saying that."

I shrug. "We won't know unless we try. But we gotta move or we'll miss the window."

Jonah hesitates. "Fiiiiiiine," he says, finally getting out of bed. "But I'm not changing. It's pj's or bust."

"Okay," I say, grabbing his hoodie from the hook on his door. "But take this. Fairy tales can be chilly."

"Prince," Jonah whisper-calls. "Come on, boy."

Our super-adorable dog, Prince, wakes up from where he was sleeping in the corner of Jonah's room. He bounds over to us, tail wagging. Prince always comes with us into fairy tales. We found him in *Sleeping Beauty*, but that's a whole other story.

Jonah and I tiptoe past our parents' room and down the stairs. I grab my sneakers from the hall and throw my brother his. We lace them up and then hurry down the steps to the basement, Prince fast on our heels.

The mirror — it's a little bigger than I am — is bolted to the wall. The frame is made out of stone and etched with fairies and wands. I study myself in the mirror: I also have bedhead, so I try to smooth my brown curls into place.

It's time to knock.

"You can have the honors," I tell Jonah.

"Whatever," he says, his voice low and lacking enthusiasm. He knocks on the mirror. Once. It hisses. Twice. It turns purple. Three times. It starts to swirl.

"It's working!" I cheer. "Hurrah!"

"Hurrah," he mutters, rolling his eyes. "There's no way we're going to end up in *Jack and the Beanstalk.* Just saying."

"Oh, hush. This is gonna be fun." I take Jonah's hand and squeeze it as we jump through.

THUD.

We land on a patch of hay in what seems to be a small barn. Its walls are made of weathered wood. And it definitely smells like a barn — like when you visit a petting zoo. I don't see any animals, though.

Is there a barn in *Jack and the Beanstalk*?

Please let there be a barn in *Jack and the Beanstalk*.

Prince gets up and starts sniffing the one corral, which is empty. Jonah stands up and stretches and pulls hay off his pj's. He sighs loudly. He's clearly not cheered up yet.

Through the small window, light spills into the barn. I stand up to look outside. It's daytime, but overcast and foggy.

"I bet you don't see a beanstalk," Jonah says grumpily.

"Um . . . I don't," I admit. All I can see is a very small house. It's made of the same weathered brown wood as the barn and has a brick chimney on the roof. The house and barn are surrounded by a rickety brown fence and, beyond that, rolling green hills. "But we're somewhere in the country. Beanstalks grow in the country!" I add hopefully.

Prince barks, as if he agrees.

Jonah groans. "Forget it. We're definitely not in *Jack and the Beanstalk*. Maybe Maryrose can let us go back now — "

Moo! Mooo!

I freeze. A cow! I just heard a cow moo from somewhere outside! At least I think it was a cow. Nothing else makes a moo sound.

There is definitely a cow in *Jack and the Beanstalk.* It's one of the most important parts of the story!

"Did you hear that, Jonah?" I ask excitedly. "Did you? It's a cow! It mooed!"

"So what?" Jonah says, but there's a teeny bit of interest in his voice.

I move around to the other end of the window, and I see something! Yes!

A skinny woman about my mom's age is sitting on a stool in front of a super-skinny brown cow. The woman is wearing a tattered gray dress and threadbare brown shoes. A yellow bandana is tied around her head and she's holding a tin pail under the cow.

"Come on, Princess Milka," the woman says to the cow. "Be a love and give us some milk, will ya?"

My eyes widen. "Jonah, come see!" I hiss, and he hurries over to join me by the window.

We watch the woman squeeze the cow's udders like I've seen farmers do at the state fair. I, personally, have never milked a cow. And I am not sure I ever want to.

"Is the cow named Princess Milka in *Jack and the Beanstalk*?" Jonah whispers.

I try to remember the story from when our nana read it to us. "Princess Milka doesn't sound familiar. But I don't know. There are a few versions of *Jack and the Beanstalk*," I say. I know the basic story, but I haven't read it in a while. Don't tell Jonah.

Moo, the cow says again. *Moooooooo.*

The woman sighs. "Not a drop of milk out of ya — for the seventh day in a row!" she groans. "Your milk was all we had to sell at the market for money. Now what'll we do? We have no money and very little food left. I'll have to sell you."

"She'll have to sell her!" I say to Jonah. "Did you hear that? That is exactly what happens in *Jack and the Beanstalk.* Exactly! Jack's mom wants to sell the cow. That must be Jack's mom." I grab my brother's arm. "Jonah, we're in the story! We have to be!"

Jonah's eyes are the size of saucers. "Are you sure?"

I don't want to promise anything yet, but it seems VERY likely.

Then we both hear the woman say, "I'll ask Jack to take you to the market, Princess Milka."

JACK?

She said Jack!

Jonah and I gasp at the same time, and glance at each other. We did it! We're in *Jack and the Beanstalk.* For real! Wahoo!

"I can't believe it," Jonah whispers. "We're really here."

"Come on," I say happily. "Let's go introduce ourselves. We can ask to meet Jack!"

I open the door to the barn and step outside. The weather is weird. It's neither warm nor cold and there's a mist in the air — not quite a drizzle like you'd need a raincoat, but my curly hair is probably getting even curlier from all the humidity.

I expect Jonah to run over to the woman. To hurl himself at her. To fly. This is it. We're going to meet Jack.

But Jonah freezes in the doorway. He takes a step back. And another step.

"No," he says.

Huh?

"I don't . . . I don't want to meet Jack," he says. With a jolt, he turns around and disappears into the barn.

chapter three

But It's Jack!

I follow Jonah back inside the barn.

"What's going on?" I ask. "Meeting Jack is your dream!"

"It is," he says with a big sigh. He sits down on the hay, knees tucked into his chest. Prince comes over and nuzzles him.

"So . . ." I prompt.

"I don't want what always happens to happen," Jonah says, shaking his head again and again.

"What always happens?" I ask.

He throws his hands up in the air. "We change the story!"

He has a point. We don't change the stories on *purpose*. At least, not usually. But we do always change them.

"Yeah," I say. "I guess we do."

"And I don't want to change *Jack and the Beanstalk*," he says. "It's perfect as it is!"

Ah. Now I get it.

"Aww, Jonah, things usually turn out just fine," I soothe him. "Even better, actually!"

He kicks a piece of hay with his foot. "You saw what happened at soccer today. I messed up. I mess up everything lately. And I don't want to mess up Jack." He puts his head down on his knees.

"You do not mess everything up," I say. "It was just one game! And, well, we ARE already here," I point out. "And maybe we could be super careful? See how it goes? We don't want to just hide in the barn. And I know you'll regret not meeting Jack. You really will."

He bites his lower lip. "Yeah. I probably would."

"You definitely would. C'mon, stand up." I take his hands and pull him to his feet.

"We have to be SUPER careful," Jonah says. "'Kay? I don't want to do anything wrong. Jack is . . . is . . . my hero."

"Really?" I say. That seems a *little* extreme.

Jonah nods. "Yes. He is. He's so brave. And a good climber. And he's not scared of anything! He's like the big brother I've always wanted."

I bristle. "Big brother? A big sister isn't good enough?" I'm definitely brave. And if I do say so myself, I've gotten to be a pretty good climber thanks to all the fairy tales we've visited. I don't exactly love heights, but I climbed up Rapunzel's braid without too much of a problem. (Jonah's the one who messed up her hair.)

Jonah flushes. "A sister is good, too! You know what I mean."

I don't really, but I don't want to argue with Jonah now. "So should we go say hi?" I ask.

"Yes!"

After all this, we better really be in Jack's story. There better not be a Jill hanging around here somewhere, ready to fetch a pail of water and roll down a hill.

Jonah slides open the barn door, and Prince follows us outside.

It has started to drizzle, so I put my hood on. Jonah does the same. See, I knew hoodies were a good idea.

We walk over to the woman. "Um, hello?" I say.

She practically jumps at the sound of my voice. "Hullo there," she says. "You surprised me. We don't get many visitors this far from town." She has an accent that makes her sound kind of like Mary Poppins. British.

Moooo, the cow says, swishing her tail. Prince barks at the cow in a friendly way.

"I'm Abby, and this is my brother, Jonah," I say. "That's our dog, Prince."

"I'm called Ada," the woman says. "And this is Princess Milka." She pats the cow's side. "Are you friends of Jack's?" Ada asks us.

Jonah and I turn to each other, our eyes wide. Jonah is jumping on his toes.

"Yes," Jonah says. "Well, kind of. He doesn't know us. We're just visiting."

"Visiting Tradetown?" the woman scoffs. "Not much to see here besides a few shops and the market."

The drizzle gets harder. Raindrops land on my nose and hands.

“Why don’t you kids come in out of the rain?” Ada suggests. “You’re going to get your clothes all wet. Jack should be home soon, and you can stay for lunch.”

She is inviting us in! Jack’s mother is inviting us in! This is it! I’ve never seen Jonah grin so big, not even when he gets extra ketchup with his French fries at the diner.

After Ada returns Princess Milka to the barn, she leads us inside the house. It’s very spare. There are four rickety chairs around a peeling wood table, an ancient-looking sofa, and a fireplace. Prince curls up on the patchy rug to take a nap. That dog can sleep anywhere.

“I’ll be making the pottage now,” Ada says. “It’s not much, but it’s hot and filling nonetheless. You two make yourselves at home and warm your bones by the fire.”

“Thank you,” I say, taking off my damp hoodie. I turn to Jonah. “Any idea what pottage is?”

He shrugs and takes off his hoodie, too. “Something cooked in a pot?”

“Helpful,” I say. I lay our hoodies near the fire to dry. Then we sit cross-legged on the rug next to where Prince is sleeping.

I spot a clock on the wall. It's 1:10 P.M. And we've been here for . . . a little over an hour already? So it was 12:00 P.M. when we arrived here. And my watch says it's 12:10 A.M. at home. So that means . . . well, I don't know what it means! I'll have to check the time again later.

"I wonder where Jack is," Jonah says impatiently, rubbing his hands together.

"Me too," I say. "In the version of the story I remember, I think he's just home with his mom all the time."

"Is that the version with the fairy?" Jonah asks.

I tilt my head. Fairy? There's no fairy in *Jack and the Beanstalk*.

"The version I know doesn't have a fairy," I say.

Jonah smiles. "The version *I* know does!" he says.

"Really? Tell it to me," I say.

This is a first. I'm always the one telling my brother the stories. But Jonah is kind of an expert on *Jack and the Beanstalk*.

He clears his throat and sits up straight. He looks quite proud. "Once upon a time, there was a boy named Jack. He and his mom lived in a little house in the countryside. They were very poor. All they had for money was a cow whose milk they sold at the market."

"Princess Milka!" I say.

Jonah nods. "So one day," he continues, "the mom realizes that the cow isn't giving milk anymore. No milk means they don't have anything to sell at the market for money."

Right. That's where we are in the story. We haven't messed anything up yet. Yay, us.

"So what do they do?" I ask.

Jonah furrows his brow and thinks. And thinks. A full minute passes.

"Oh, yeah, I remember the order now," he says. "The mom tells Jack to bring the cow to the market and sell it. So Jack starts the long walk to the market with the cow. On the way, a man stops Jack and says he'll trade Jack magic beans for the cow. Jack loves magic. So he says yes to the trade."

I wonder if I would have done the same thing in that situation. I mean, magic beans? Who can resist?

"But when Jack gets home with the beans, all excited," Jonah goes on, "his mom is so mad that he got tricked into giving away their cow. She says there's no such thing as magic beans. The mom sends poor Jack to bed without any dinner — ”

“No pottage for him!” I say.

Jonah frowns. “Now I know how it feels when I’m always interrupting you.”

“Hah! Sorry.” I snort-laugh and zip my lips.

“And then the mom tosses the beans out the window. But guess what happens in the morning?”

“What?” I ask, even though of course I already know.

“A giant beanstalk grew out of those beans in the night!” Jonah is beaming. “The beanstalk is so tall it goes right up through the clouds! Cool, right? I would LOVE to climb a giant beanstalk. If we really are in the story, do you think we’ll get to climb it? Do you?”

“Of course,” I say. “But go on! Get to the fairy part.”

“So,” Jonah continues, “Jack climbs up the beanstalk. And up. And up. AND UP. He’s so high up in the sky that he’s above the clouds. And then he sees a castle.”

I wonder if the castle feels sturdy. Without a ground. I’m not sure how it could. Is it resting on the clouds? What happens when it rains? What happens *after* it rains?

"Abby, please pay attention," Jonah tells me.

"Sorry," I say, focusing back on Jonah.

"So Jack goes inside and meets a giant woman. She's a million feet tall."

I raise an eyebrow. "A million?"

"At least. And she tells Jack he'd better leave because her husband, the giant, eats little boys as a snack. He's sleeping now but if he wakes up . . ."

I shudder.

"Anyway, Jack tells her he's starving because he didn't have dinner. The lady giant offers Jack some cheese and bread and says to eat fast and then leave."

"Does he?"

Jonah nods. "Well, he eats, but he doesn't leave. Want to know why?"

"Why?"

"Because the giant wakes up! And he starts sniffing the air. Then he sings a song: 'FEE, FI, FO, FUM. I smell the blood of an Englishman!' There's more to the song . . . something about bread." Jonah shrugs. "Anyway, Jack hides and watches as the giant sits down to a meal and starts counting his gold coins. He has bags full of them.

Jack knows that if he takes a bag of gold coins home to his mother, she won't be mad at him anymore. And they'll never be hungry again."

"But how does he take one when the giant is counting his coins?" I ask.

"The giant falls asleep — right at the table," Jonah explains. "And Jack rushes out of his hiding place, grabs a bag of coins, and flees the castle! He goes racing down the beanstalk."

"Does the giant chase him?" I ask.

"Nope," Jonah says. "He's fast asleep. When Jack tells his mom what happened and shows her the coins, she's so happy! They can now buy food and new shoes and comfortable chairs."

I fidget on my very stiff chair, and nod.

"Plus, a new cow," Jonah says. "Maybe even two new cows!"

"Well, that's a relief for them," I say.

"But eventually the money runs out," Jonah goes on. "Jack has no choice but to go back up the beanstalk for more coins. The lady giant recognizes him right away and tells him to scram. She says the giant noticed the missing bag of coins, and if he catches Jack . . . *whooo boy.*" Then Jonah scratches his head, as if trying to remember what happens next.

Thirty seconds go by. Then a minute. I sigh. "Something about a goose that lays golden eggs?" I prompt him.

Jonah's eyes light up. "That's right — the goose! Okay, so Jack sneaks back into the giants' castle. He watches the man giant tell his goose to lay a golden egg. And the goose does! A golden egg! When the giant falls asleep again, Jack grabs the goose and races down the beanstalk with it. The goose lays a golden egg right in their little house. Soon, Jack and his mom are richer than ever!" Jonah tilts his head again. "I forget the goose's name."

"I think it's just the goose that lays the golden eggs."

He scrunches up his face. "But I feel like I'm forgetting something else." He scratches his head again and sticks out his tongue in concentration.

"Where does the fairy come in?" I ask.

"Oh, yeah!" Jonah says. "That's what I forgot! At some point, a fairy tells Jack that the giant is the one who killed Jack's dad and stole his dad's money. It's the reason why Jack and his mom are so poor."

"What?" I ask, surprised. "The giant killed Jack's dad? That's horrible!" I knew Jack's mom was a widow, but I don't remember ever hearing what happened to his dad.

"So," Jonah continues, "even though Jack and his mom are rich because of the golden eggs from the goose, Jack wants to go back up to the giant's castle *again* and see what else he might want."

"That sounds a little greedy," I say. "But okay."

"Yeah, but the mean giant killed his dad and stole their family's money," Jonah reminds me. "So maybe the giant deserves it."

"Fair enough," I say. "So Jack goes back up the beanstalk?"

Jonah nods. "The lady giant sees him and says the man giant is REALLY mad. But Jack doesn't care. He hides and sees the giant telling a golden harp to play a song. And it does. Boy, does Jack want that harp. I mean, can you blame him? So he steals it and runs. But this time, the giant wakes up and sees him! He tells Jack to come back with his harp. Jack doesn't — he keeps running and goes climbing down the beanstalk as fast as he can. The giant is climbing down after him. The beanstalk is shaking like crazy. Jack calls out, 'Mom, get your ax, chop down the beanstalk! The giant is coming!'"

Yup, that's how it goes in the version I know, too.

"So the mom chops down the beanstalk," Jonah says, "and the giant falls off the beanstalk and lands with a thud and that's the end of him." Jonah makes a cutting motion across his neck.

"Oof," I say. "Then do Jack and his mom live happily ever after?"

"They do," Jonah says. "Jack marries a princess, too."

"Really?"

He nods.

"This town has a princess?"

Jonah shrugs. "I guess?"

"How old is Jack anyway?"

He shrugs again.

I smell something good coming from the kitchen. My stomach rumbles.

"Just a few minutes till lunch is ready," Ada calls out. "I sure hope Jack gets home soon. It's raining something fierce out there."

I hear footsteps running outside. Toward the house.

I look at Jonah, and then we both stare at the door.

Will it be Jack? It has to be Jack. Please be Jack!

The door opens, and a boy walks in. He looks older than me, maybe twelve or thirteen. He's tall and skinny with a mop of light brown hair and hazel-green eyes. His shirt is wet from the rain and tattered like his mom's dress, and his thin pants are way too short. He's wearing really scuffed-up sneakers with big holes. I can see one toe sticking out. The other sneaker is held together with black tape.

His eyes widen when he sees us. "Uh, who are you two?" he asks. He also has a British accent.

"We're Abby and Jonah," I say. "And that's Prince, our dog. And you are?"

I hold my breath.

The boy smiles. "Nice to meet you, mates. I'm Jack."

chapter four

Spilling the Beans

Jonah's eyes are lit up like lightbulbs. He jumps to his feet and runs over to Jack, flinging his arms around him. "Jack!" he cries. "I've been waiting to meet you forever."

Jack looks surprised, taking a step back. "Me? Well, that's a first."

I get up and walk over to them.

"Jonah, let him go," I say, because Jonah is still hugging Jack tight. Thankfully, Jonah listens to me and drops his arms.

Prince wakes up and runs over to Jack. He starts to sniff his falling-apart sneakers.

"How do you know me?" Jack asks, looking from Jonah to me in confusion.

Before Jonah or I can explain, Ada comes out of the kitchen.

"There you are, Jack!" Ada says, holding a pot with both hands. "I thought I'd have to keep lunch warm for you."

"Sorry," Jack says. "I was playing football near the market and lost track of time, but then the rain started."

"You play football?" Jonah asks. "I don't. But I play soccer. Not well."

"Jonah," I whisper. "I think this place is like England. I bet they call soccer *foot*ball here."

Jonah grins. "Oh! Cool!"

Jack nods. "I'm really good at football. I can give you some pointers after lunch if the rain stops, Jonah."

"Awesome!" Jonah says. He looks happy. No. He looks ecstatic. I remember what he said earlier about Jack being the big brother he's always dreamed of, and I feel a funny twinge.

Am I a little jealous? Of Jack?

No. Maybe.

Ada sets the pot down on the table, and Jonah, Jack, and I sit down in the chairs. Jonah makes sure to sit next to Jack, gazing up at him admiringly.

"Jack," Ada says, "when it stops raining, I'll need you to take Princess Milka to the market and sell her for a good price. She's not giving any more milk."

"I'm sorry to hear that, Mum. But I can do that if you need me to," Jack responds.

Aw. Jack seems sweet. And I can't help but notice — he's kind of . . . cute. I like the way his golden-brown bangs flop over his forehead. And he has a nice smile. His accent doesn't hurt, either. I shake my head, trying to push these thoughts away.

I'm in a fairy tale. I need to focus.

"I just have to tape my right sneaker before I go," Jack is saying. "The sole completely came off. My foot got soaked."

Ada frowns. "If you get a good price for the cow, you can buy yourself some decent used sneakers from the thrift stall at the market."

Wow. So sad. I feel lucky that I never have to worry about having money for food or new shoes.

"Thanks, Mum," Jack says.

"Abby?" Jonah whispers. "What's a mum?"

"It's how they say 'mom' here," I explain.

"Ohhh," he says. "Now I get it."

Ada is about to sit down at the table, when she smacks her palm against her forehead. "I forgot the plates and spoons. Where is my head?" she asks. "Too worried about money troubles — that's where."

When Ada goes back into the kitchen, Jonah turns to Jack excitedly.

"Jack," Jonah whispers. "Guess what?"

"What?" Jack asks.

Jonah has a huge smile on his face. "After lunch, you won't have to worry about holes in your sneakers ever again."

Uh-oh. What's he doing?

"Huh?" Jack asks. "Why not?"

"On the way to the market," Jonah begins, "you're gonna meet a man who'll trade you magic beans for Princess Milka!"

No, Jonah, no!

Jack laughs. "Magic beans? I would never sell our only cow for 'magic' anything. You're funny."

"No, I'm serious!" Jonah assures him. "You WANT to make the trade for the beans. You'll end up with gold coins and —"

"Jonah!" I whisper. I reach across the table to nudge his arm. "Don't . . . spill the beans!"

"Ha!" Jonah says.

"What beans?" asks Jack, looking confused.

"No beans," I say. "Let's not talk about beans."

"Doesn't the word 'beans' sound like a word you'd say when you mess up something?" Jonah asks. "Like, I just broke a glass. Oh, beans!"

"Jack!" Ada calls from the kitchen. "Come carry the plates and glasses."

"Sure thing, Mum," Jack responds, leaping up to help her.

I turn to my brother. "What are you doing? You said you wanted to be super careful."

"I am! I'm being careful not to mess it up. But I can tell him what happens — 'cause it happens!"

"It's just better not to say anything," I say. "Fairy tales are tricky. You never know what can mess it up."

Jonah covers his mouth with his hand.

Ada and Jack come back to the table. Jack sets out the plates and glasses.

"Oh, Mum, listen to this," Jack says. "Jonah told me that on the way to the market I'm going to meet a trader who'll sell me beans for Princess Milka. He says the beans are magic! How fun is that?"

"WHAT?" Ada shrieks. "Absolutely not! There is no such thing as magic beans!"

Crumbs.

She shakes her head. "There are lots of scammers at the market these days. You know what, Jack, you stay home and play with your new friends. I'll take the cow to the market myself. No one will try to rip me off." She shakes her head with a grim laugh.

Oh, no. Oh no oh no oh no.

"Sounds good, Mum," Jack says, digging into his food.

And there we have it. The trickiness in action. We've been here for ten minutes, and we've already messed up the story.

I shoot a look at Jonah.

"Beans," he says.

* * *

The pottage turns out to be a vegetable stew. The portions are small because there's so little of it to go around. How nice is Jack's family that they're sharing their food with us when they have so little? That makes me feel even worse about messing up their story.

Jonah makes sad faces at me while we eat, so I whisper, "We'll fix it. Don't worry."

After we're done eating, we help Ada clear the table. Then Jonah, Prince, Jack, and I head into the tiny living room. I glance at Jack. He doesn't look upset about not being able to get gold coins. He probably doesn't realize that it was true. I watch as he does some pretty fancy footwork with his soccer ball.

"Jack's so good at footie I don't even mind him playing in the house," Ada says, smiling at him as she heads to the kitchen.

Jonah is mesmerized by the shabby, scuffed ball at Jack's feet. "How'd you get so good at soccer — I mean, football?" Jonah asks Jack.

"My dad taught me when I was small," Jack responds. "We played all the time. But then he died."

"Sorry," Jonah and I say at the same time.

"I get sad if I talk about my father too much," Jack adds. "So I try not to."

Poor Jack. That horrible giant killed his dad and stole his money, leaving Jack and his mother with nothing. And now we've made it worse for them.

Prince barks, trying to chase the ball that's under Jack's feet. Jack laughs, crouching down to pet him. "You have the cutest dog," Jack says.

Woof! Prince agrees. He rolls over on his back and Jack gives him a tummy rub.

Awww. Could Jack BE any sweeter?

And did I mention how cute he is?

"I wish we could have a dog, but we can barely feed ourselves," Jack says. He pets Prince's floppy ears.

Poor Jack. I glance at Jonah. He looks as miserable as I feel. We have to fix this somehow.

"Jack, honey, come help me put the heavy pot in the sink," Ada calls from the kitchen.

Jack gives the ball a gentle kick over to Jonah and goes into the kitchen.

As soon as Jack is gone, Jonah turns to me, his eyes troubled.

"Told you I mess everything up!" Jonah cries. "I wish we'd never gone into this story. I ruined everything for Jack!"

"Shhh," I say. "Listen . . ." I trail off.

But what is there to say? Jonah kind of did mess up by, yes, spilling the beans. About the beans.

"Now Jack won't get the magic beans," Jonah adds, his voice rising. "And that means no beanstalk, no giant, no gold coins, no goose that lays golden eggs, and no magic harp. They'll be poor forever."

He's right. But I can't tell him that since he feels bad enough.

And I kind of feel like the giant OWES Jack.

"We'll come up with a solution," I tell my brother.

We HAVE to.

I stare out the window at the drizzle, thinking. If only there was a way to get the beans ourselves. That would solve everything, right? We'd get the beans, give them to Jack, and —

Ahhh!

Ding, ding, ding! I got it!

chapter five

A Fair Trade

"I figured it out," I say.

Jonah's eyes widen. "How?"

"Well, we know there's someone out there trading magic beans," I say. "We just have to find the trader ourselves and trade him *something* for the beans! Then *we'll* have the beans. Get it?"

"Got it!" Jonah cries. "And then we'll give the beans to Jack!"

I nod. If we get those beans, Jack will get his gold coins. And his mom can buy another cow. And sturdy chairs. And new sneakers for Jack. YAY!

Ada and Jack come out of the kitchen, and Ada glances out the window. "Good. The rain stopped. I need to get Princess Milka to the market to sell her."

"We don't mind taking her," I say quickly.

"No, I've got it," she insists. "I want to make sure it's done properly. No silly magic beans. It's the only way we'll survive. See you later, Jack," she says, kissing his cheek.

"Bye, Mum," he says with a smile. He tosses his mop of brown bangs out of his eyes.

Ada waves to us and leaves. I look out the window and see her walking down the path, holding on to Princess Milka's rope. The cow gives a moo as she walks slowly beside Ada.

As soon as they're out of sight, I turn to Jack and Jonah.

"So here's what we have to do," I say. "We have to find the man who has the magic beans and trade him something else for them."

Jack frowns. "What do you mean? You were serious about those beans?"

"Very serious," I say with a nod. "Trust us."

"You have to get those beans," Jonah tells Jack. "Your whole life will change!"

"Really?" Jack asks. "How?"

"You'll get gold coins and a goose that lays golden eggs, plus a magic harp," Jonah says. "You'll be rich!"

Jack smiles. "Rich? I'll settle for not starving." He rubs his stomach. "I could have eaten another helping of pottage. Sure would be nice to have some extra potatoes every week."

I realize he's not exaggerating when he says he's starving. He really is.

We're getting those beans for Jack. We ARE!

"What can we trade?" Jonah asks, looking around.

"Mum took the cow," Jack says. "All I have is the clothes on my back, and nobody wants those. They're too shabby."

"*Our* clothes are in good shape!" Jonah says. He points to his pajamas. "Right, Abby?" He nods at my jeans.

"Um, we need to keep our clothes," I tell my brother.

"Even our hoodies?" he asks.

"Yes," I say. The last thing I need is Jonah catching a cold in a fairy tale.

"But then we don't have anything to trade!" Jonah cries.

True. Very unfortunately true.

Oh, wait.

We DO have something to trade.

I look down at my watch.

If we want to save the story, I have to sell it.

"What?" Jonah asks.

I lift up my wrist and point to my watch.

"No! How will we know what time it is back home?" Jonah asks.

I look at my watch. It's twelve thirty at home now. Then I check the clock in Jack's living room. It's three thirty here. So . . . that means every half hour at home is about three and half hours here. So every hour at home is about seven hours here. I do the calculations.

"So seven A.M. at home is one P.M. here the day after tomorrow. We'll want to leave here by noon. Latest," I tell Jonah. "And I got the watch in a goody bag from a party. It's a cheap one. I can get another one in Smithville." It wouldn't be the first watch I've lost in a fairy tale.

"Are you sure, Abby?" Jack asks me, looking at the watch. "It has sparkles on it! I've never seen a watch with sparkles on it! It's beautiful."

I blush. Then I remind myself that Jack said the *watch* was beautiful. Not me!

Oh, no. I teased Jonah for having a crush on Little Red Riding Hood. Do I maybe . . . have a crush on Jack?

But there's no time to wonder about that. We have to find the trader, and fast.

"I'm sure," I say. "Let's head for the market. We should see the trader on the way there."

Jonah, Jack, and I hurry out the door, with Prince following behind.

Jack leads us down a gravel road toward the market. The sky is still overcast and there's that mist in the air, but at least it's not raining. Soon, we reach a small village. The stone buildings are small and very close together and almost look like mini castles. There are curving cobblestone streets and alleyways and lots of shops. And a few blocks farther up is the market. There are open-air stalls and people milling around, buying and selling stuff. And is that fish and chips I smell? YUM. My stomach grumbles. Maybe I should trade my watch for something to eat instead. Kidding. Kind of.

"I see my mum!" Jack says, peering ahead. "She's standing right outside the market talking to a man!"

Hmmm. Could the man she's talking to be the trader?

We sneak behind a tree and watch. Yep, there's Ada, still holding on to Princess Milka. A tall, thin man with curly hair is showing Ada something he has in the palm of his hand.

The beans! He must be showing her the beans! And telling her they're magic!

I see Ada shake her head with a laugh and wag her finger at the trader. She walks on with the cow into the market, and then I lose sight of her.

"That has to be the trader," I say, watching the curly-haired man.

"Let's go talk to him!" Jonah says, darting forward.

"Wait," I say, grabbing hold of him.

"What's wrong?" Jack asks me.

"I think we should let the trader approach US," I say. "Like in the story."

"What story?" Jack asks, looking from me to Jonah and back to me.

Oops. Think fast, Abby. "Oh, um, I just mean we heard that he'll trade the beans for something he sees that he wants."

"Ah," Jack says. "I have an idea! As we walk near him, hold out your wrist so he can see the watch, Abby."

"Brilliant!" Jonah says. "You are SO smart, Jack."

"Thanks," Jack says with a smile.

I frown. Jack *is* smart. But I'm the one who came up with this whole plan in the first place.

"Are you sure you don't mind giving up your watch, Abby?" Jack asks me. "I feel bad about it."

"It's okay," I say.

"You'll get another watch, right?" Jack asks me. "You can wish on the magic beans and ask for whatever you want, right? Isn't that how the magic beans work?"

Jonah and I exchange a glance. "Not exactly," Jonah says. "The beans will help you find the gold coins and then you can buy stuff."

Jack tilts his head. "But where will we find the gold coins?"

"One step at a time," I say, and take a deep breath.

We walk toward the trader. All around us are horse-drawn carriages and wagons and people wearing cloaks — some fancy and some tattered. There are definitely some rich people in Tradetown and some very poor people.

As we near the trader, I hold my watch up toward my face.

"Oh, my," I say loudly. "According to my watch, it's almost time to head home."

Yeah, I sound totally natural. NOT.

"Good thing you have your super-awesome watch!" Jonah shouts. "Your super-duper awesome watch!" he adds at the top of his lungs.

Not the most subtle.

But it's working! The trader is coming over to us!

"Hello," he says to me with a friendly smile. He has warm brown eyes, olive skin, and lots of curly brown hair. He looks like he's my dad's age. "My name is Devin. I'm a trader here at the market."

I offer a polite smile. "I'm Abby, and this is my brother, Jonah, and our friend Jack. And that's our dog, Prince."

"Hello," Devin says, smiling at the boys and Prince. He kneels down and gives Prince a pat on the head, then stands back up. Now his eyes are on my wrist. "That's a nice watch. It sparkles."

Yes! Our plan worked! "Thanks," I say. "I'd love to trade my watch for something special. But we don't see anything all that interesting around here. Just the usual stuff." La, la la.

Devin glances around, then turns his attention back to me. "I DO happen to have something very interesting to trade."

"What?" Jonah asks with complete curiosity. Either he's a brilliant actor or he actually has forgotten.

"Magic beans," Devin whispers. He has them in his palm and holds out his hand so we can see. They look like ordinary greenish-brown beans. There are four of them. He tosses one up in the air and catches it.

"What's so magical about them?" Jack asks.

"Where they are planted, a beanstalk will grow, straight up into the sky past the clouds," Devin says. "Climb the beanstalk and riches await you."

I wouldn't believe him if I didn't know it was true. I stare at my watch. *Good-bye, watch. Thanks for all the time-telling on my adventures!*

"Okay," I say. "I'll trade you my watch for the beans." I unstrap the watch and hold it out to Devin.

He shakes his head. "So sorry, but I am not interested in your watch."

"What?" I exclaim. "What do you mean you don't want the watch?"

Devin holds up his wrist. "I have my own."

Oh.

Crumbs.

Now what?

Jonah's face crumples. He seriously looks like he might cry. He shoves his hands in his hoodie pockets.

"Hey, what's this?" Jonah says, trying to pull something out.

"Huh?" I ask. "What's what?"

Ugh. Jonah probably has melty, half-crushed M&M's in his pocket from weeks ago. But who knows? Maybe Devin likes chocolate.

"I didn't know I had this!" Jonah exclaims, and pulls out his e-reader.

Crazy! "You had an e-reader in your hoodie pocket and didn't know it?" I ask.

Jonah shrugs. "I love my e-reader so much I always have it in my pocket."

Devin's eyes light up. "Let me see that, young man." He holds out his hand.

Jonah's mouth drops open, and he takes a step back. "This? No. Not this!"

“Seriously, Jonah?” I say.

“I can’t trade my e-reader!” he yelps. “What would I tell Mom and Dad?”

“Wow,” Jack says, staring at the e-reader in wonder. “I’ve never seen that before. How cool. What does it do?”

“You read on it,” Jonah tells him.

“They definitely don’t sell those around here. You’re so lucky you have one. You definitely *can’t* sell that,” Jack says.

Jonah hesitates. He hands the e-reader to the trader. “No. Take it. I can . . . I’ll tell Mom and Dad I lost it. I’m sure they’ll get me another one . . . when I turn thirty, maybe.” He mumbles the last part. “Mr. Trader, I will trade you. My e-reader for those magic beans.”

Aw, I’m so proud of my little brother. GO, JONAH!

“Oh, I don’t want *that*,” Devin says. He shakes his head and turns away.

“WHAT?” I shriek.

Devin turns back around. “I’m not much of a reader,” he says. “I prefer to spend my spare time playing Scrabble or chess.”

And making trading really difficult.

"Wait," I say in desperation. "How about our hoodies?" I gesture at my red one and Jonah's orange one. "They're super soft." And all we have left.

Devin shakes his head. "I have a closetful."

Jonah's shoulders slump again.

"Well, that's it," I say, throwing up my hands. "We're out of stuff to sell. We have nothing else to trade."

"What a cute dog," the trader says. "Look at those floppy ears."

We all look. Prince's ears *are* especially cute.

Devin kneels down in front of our dog. "Come here, boy," he says to Prince.

Prince pads over and sits. He gives the trader's hand a lick.

Devin laughs. "What a good dog," he says, and pats Prince on the head.

Then the trader stands up. "You've got your trade. The magic beans for your dog."

chapter six

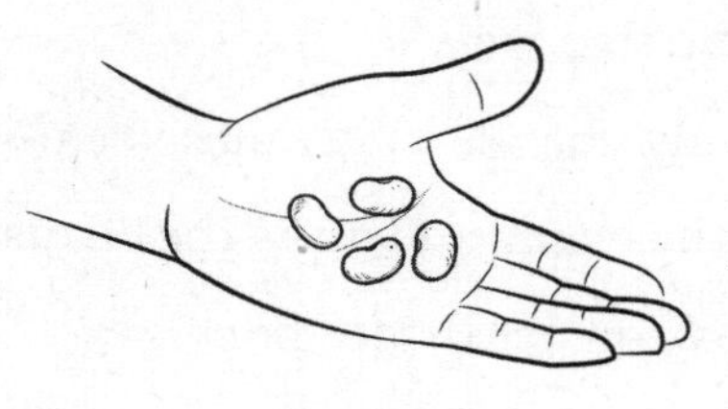

Ruff!

Wait, what?

He didn't just . . . ?

No way.

I walk in front of Prince and make sure he's behind my legs. "Prince is NOT for sale," I say sternly.

"Oh," Devin says. "I thought you wanted the beans."

"Prince is our *dog*," I say. "He's part of our *family*."

Jonah nods. "It's SO true. He's like the little brother I don't have."

I glance at Jonah. "Why do you keep wishing for brothers?"

"How about this," Devin says. "I'll let you buy him back for only ten gold coins whenever you want."

I hesitate. No. No way.

"It's your only chance to get these beans," Devin adds.

If we plant the beans and grow the beanstalk, we can get those gold coins and get Prince back.

I look at Jonah. He looks at Prince. Prince's tail wags as he looks up at Devin. He seems to *like* him. But my heart breaks at the thought of anything happening to Prince. I can't leave him! What if something goes wrong?

Talk about a tough choice. A total dilemma. I think back to how stressed I was about choosing between Frankie and Robin. This is even tougher! Much tougher.

"Guys, you're not trading Prince for some plain old beans," Jack says, stepping forward. "My mum was right. We're being ridiculous. There's no such thing as magic beans. And super-poor families like me and my mum don't get rich overnight. Trust me, I wish we could, but it doesn't happen."

Sigh. Why does Jack have to be so nice? If only he were a jerk, I could grab Jonah and Prince and make a run for it. I'd find the portal back home and leave this fairy tale behind.

But no. When we're in fairy tales, we have to help, no matter what. That's why Maryrose sends us into the stories in the first place. To help. I think, anyway. Or it might just be to train us for a mission. We're not exactly sure.

Jonah's lip quivers. I know he doesn't want to let Jack down.

Jack puts his arm around Jonah's shoulders. "Don't worry, Jonah. Me and my mum will get by. I'll drop out of school and try to find work here in town. I'm too young for a proper job, but someone might pay me a bit to run errands or something."

No. He can't drop out of school. He just can't.

Jonah looks miserable.

"Children," the trader says with a smile. "I'll make you a special deal."

I narrow my eyes. "What kind of deal?" I ask.

"I will give you the magic beans," Devin begins. "You give me your dog. If you return with *five* gold coins, not ten, you can trade in your dog. No problem."

Five coins to get Prince back. Jack won't have to drop out of school. Jonah won't be miserable forever. And Ada can buy a thousand cows with the riches those beans will provide.

I stare at Devin. "Five gold coins? And you'll give Prince back to us?"

"Swearsies. You two heard the deal," Devin says to Jack and Jonah.

I can't believe I'm even considering this, but . . .

"Uh, give us a minute, will you?" I say to Jack and the trader. I pull Jonah aside.

"Jonah, we know that the trader is at least being honest about the beans," I start. "The beans *will* grow into a giant beanstalk high in the sky. Riches are waiting for us up there. Once we get the money, we can buy Prince back. It shouldn't take more than a few hours."

Am I actually saying this? I am.

"Trade Prince?" Jonah says, scrunching up his face.

"I know," I say. "Even for a few hours — I hate the idea."

Jonah bites his lip. "But we have to, right?"

"I think we do," I say.

Jonah looks like he might cry. "This is all my fault, Abby. If I didn't say anything about the beans to begin with, we wouldn't even be thinking about trading Prince. But if we don't trade him, Jack will always be hungry." His eyes get all misty.

Crumbs, crumbs, and more crumbs.

I bite my lip and think this over. We know there are bags and bags of gold coins in the giant's castle.

All we have to do is:

1) Plant the magic beans.
2) Wait till the beanstalk grows.
3) Climb up.
4) Sneak into the giant's castle.
5) Take a bag of gold coins without getting eaten by the giant.
6) Climb back down.
7) Chop down the beanstalk so the giant can't follow us.
8) Return to the trader with five gold coins for Prince.

And then everyone's happy. Jack will save his family. We'll save Prince. The end.

"Jack?" I call. "Can you come here, please?"

Jack comes over. Jonah, Jack, and I huddle together, and I explain the plan. Well, I leave out the part about the castle and the giant. Jonah already knows about that. And Jack — well, I'm not sure I should tell him any of the story in advance.

"So we climb a beanstalk and get rich?" Jack says. "Easy peasy! I'm so in!"

I feel a little bad about withholding major info, but there are kind of unwritten rules in fairy tale world.

Anyway, my plan sounds perfectly reasonable. Number five (take the coins without getting eaten by the giant) is a doozy, though. We'll have to be quick.

I turn to Jonah. "So we're doing this? We're trading Prince for a little while?"

Jonah nods. "We don't have a choice! And besides, Devin is being really nice to Prince. Look," he adds, pointing.

I turn around. Devin is sitting on the ground and petting Prince, who's licking his cheek. The trader is laughing. "You're the cutest!" he says to Prince. He throws a stick off to the side where there's a grassy area. Prince runs after the stick and brings it back, dropping it at Devin's feet. "Good Prince!" Devin says, giving him another pat. "Who's a good doggie-woggie? You are, that's who!" Prince licks his cheek again.

And we know he's not lying about the magic beans. So he's somewhat trustworthy.

I let out a sigh. I feel very queasy about this. "Prince does seem to like Devin. Okay, fine. But the minute we get those five coins, we're getting Prince back."

"Definitely," Jonah says.

I walk over to the trader. "We have a d-"

I'm about to say the word *deal* when I remember something. Would my parents, who are LAWYERS, make a deal without having it written and signed? Of course they wouldn't! You need a contract. A contract puts all the terms of a deal in writing. That way, no one can change their mind and say they didn't agree to this or that. Because it's right there on paper.

I clear my throat. "We have a deal IF we write out a contract and both sign it," I tell Devin.

Devin rolls his eyes. "Well, I don't have any paper on me, do *you*, little girl?" he asks.

I frown. "First of all, I'm ten, not a little girl. And second, no, I don't." Note to self: Start carrying a small notebook.

"And what about a pen?" Devin feels his pockets. "Nope, no pen."

Crumbs. Me neither.

"You have ONE second to decide if you want to make this trade," Devin says. "I'm sure another kid would want these MAGIC beans."

"Fine!" I snap. "No contract." Crumbs. "But before I hand Prince over, tell me EXACTLY where we get him back."

"Certainly," Devin says. "You can fetch him from my house. One alley on the left past the biscuit stall, house number nineteen — two twists and three turns from the road. Can't miss it."

I nod. Biscuit stall. One alley on the left. House 19. Two twists, three turns. Got it. I have a pretty good memory.

"I know where that is, Abby," Jack says. "I can help you find it."

Whew.

"So do we have a deal?" Devin asks. "Are we making this trade? Four magic beans for your dog?"

"Yes," I say, still feeling uncertain. "Until we meet you back at your house with five gold coins," I add. "Right?"

"Right," Devin says. He smiles and hands me the beans. "Excellent. Here they are."

I look at the four greenish-brown beans in my palm.

"Come, Prince," Devin says. "I'll show you to your memory-foam dog couch in my living room. I'll even buy you a liver biscuit on the way. You will live up to your name in my company."

Prince does love liver dog biscuits. And soft beds. At least he'll be getting the royal treatment during his stay in Tradetown.

Ruff! Prince says, happily following Devin.

I swallow. I can't watch Prince walk away. I can't!

I look at the beans again. "These had better really be magic," I say.

Or we'll never see Prince again.

We run all the way back to Jack's house, the three of us out of breath. That is how excited — and anxious — we are about getting the beans planted.

We go into Jack's yard and peer through the window into his house. I can see Ada in the kitchen, peeling potatoes. There's a small pile of fruits and vegetables on the counter. I also see a pair of scuffed but decent blue sneakers on a chair. Ada must have sold Princess Milka!

I bet she didn't get much money for the cow, though.

"So," I whisper to Jonah, "Jack's mom threw the beans out the window in the original story. We should plant them right here."

"Should we just throw them on the ground?" Jonah whispers back. "That's what his mom does. She didn't plant them."

I think about that. "I don't know. I guess we could. They are magic, after all."

I toss the beans on the ground. They just sit there. Nothing magic happens.

Jack comes over and stares at the beans, then at me. "Uh, no offense, Abby, but you have to plant beans if you want them to take root and grow."

Can't hurt, right?

"Okay," I say, picking up the beans. "We'll all plant them." I give one to Jack, one to Jonah, and I have two left in my hand.

"Um, Abby?" Jonah says sheepishly.

"Yes?"

"I think Jack should have the extra bean," Jonah says. "He'd have ALL the beans if we weren't here."

Jeez. I suppose.

"Fine," I mutter. I drop the second bean in Jack's palm.

We each plant our beans. Then we get up and stare at the ground.

Still nothing happening.

"So where's the sky-high beanstalk?" Jack asks. "I hope Devin wasn't lying to us."

I look up at the sky. It's not very sunny. But it's not raining, either. Don't plants need sun and water to grow? The trader didn't say anything about that.

At least it's kind of misty again. Maybe that will help water the beans.

"I think we have to wait for it to grow overnight," I say. "That's how it happens in the story." But that *does* mean we're leaving Prince on his own for the whole night!

Eep. Poor Prince. I miss him.

"WHAT story?" Jack asks me.

Oops. "Oh, just some story I read about how beanstalks grow," I say quickly.

Jonah nods. "Yeah, we just have to go to sleep, and

when we wake up . . . beanstalk city." He leans his head back, staring straight up at the sky.

Here's hoping.

Before dinner, Jack and Jonah play soccer, aka "football," in the yard. Jack's wearing his new used sneakers that Ada bought him.

"Wow, I can play even better now that my sneakers don't fall apart mid-kick," Jack says, sending the ball toward Jonah with the side of his foot. "And the tape I had to use to hold my left sneaker together always got stuck to the ball. I hated when that happened. My mum is the best for buying me these."

"You're so good at soccer you could probably play barefoot and win!" Jonah exclaims.

I roll my eyes. He's not *that* good.

But Jonah learns a ton. Jack teaches him how to use the side of the foot to kick the ball and when to use his head.

Jack even lets Jonah get two balls past him into the goal. He's so nice. And thoughtful.

And cute.

I wonder if he has a girlfriend?

Not that I care. I don't.

"Abby, come play with us!" Jack says.

"Abby doesn't like soccer!" Jonah says.

"I do, too," I say. I walk over to join them. I don't *dislike* soccer. And I'm pretty good at being a goalie, too. I stop a few balls from going into the barn by catching them.

"Not bad," Jack says to me, and I feel myself flush.

"Dinner!" Ada calls from the window. "And wash your hands!" She pokes her head out. "Oh, dear, it's starting to rain. Abby and Jonah, do you live very far? Would you two like to stay over tonight? The couch pulls out into a bed."

Yes! Perfect! Raining AND an invitation to stay over. The rain will help the beanstalk grow and when we wake up, all we have to do is go outside to climb it.

"Thanks!" I say to Ada, and head inside. "We would like to stay over. We do live very far away. Very, *very* far."

"Yay! I'm having a sleepover at Jack's!" Jonah whispers to me as we wash our hands. "He's so awesome." He dries his hands on a scratchy towel. "I hope I can get really great at soccer just like him." He races out of the tiny bathroom to find Jack.

Okay, Jack is pretty great. But does Jonah have to follow him around the house like a puppy?

Ohhhhh puppy. I cringe. Poor Prince. I hope he's okay.

We sit down at the table. Ada has made pottage again, but this time there are hunks of potatoes and other veggies. Plus, she made fresh-squeezed lemonade. Yum.

But I can't stop thinking about Prince. I'm sure he's fine. Gobbling up his liver doggie biscuits and sleeping on his memory-foam mattress. But still.

"Where's your sweet dog?" Ada asks, as if reading my mind.

"Oh, um, he's just hiding," I say. "He doesn't like the rain."

Sigh.

Finally, it's time for bed. It's been a LONG day. And Jonah, Jack, and I want to get to sleep as soon as possible so we can see if the beanstalk is there in the morning.

Ada reaches into a small closet and pulls out a thin blue blanket and two pillows. "The sofa bed isn't all that comfortable, but it'll do for a night."

"Thanks, Ada," I say. "We really appreciate it."

Jack removes the couch cushions and pulls out the bed, then sets up the blanket and pillows. "There you go."

Jonah lets out a huge yawn.

"Night, everyone," Jack says, then climbs a peeling white ladder to a small loft area. I see a thin mattress and a thin blanket and a thin pillow.

"Night, Jack," Jonah and I say at the same time.

"Good night, kids," Ada says, going into her room.

"I'm sooo sleepy," Jonah says, his eyes drifting closed.

I'm sleepy, too. I can feel my eyes getting heavier and heavier.

PLEASE let there be a beanstalk out there in the morning. Pleeease!

The next thing I know, the sun is coming through the windows. The sky is blue.

I pop out of bed. Jack comes rushing down the loft ladder. Jonah runs to the window.

"BEANSTALK!" Jonah shouts. He zips around in a circle, pumping his fists. Jack gives him two high fives.

Both of them are dancing around the living room, chanting, "Beanstalk. Beanstalk. Beanstalk!"

I stare out the window in shock. It's really there!

The beanstalk is huge. It's about three feet wide and bright green with tons of thick sprouts and stems coming out the sides. It's so tall that I can't even see the top. It shoots straight up through the clouds.

"It really worked!" I exclaim. "The magic beans grew into a giant beanstalk!"

"You know what that means," Jonah says. "Let's do some climbing!"

Chapter Seven

Into the Sky

"I wonder what riches are waiting for us up there," Jack says once we're outside. He shields his eyes from the sun as he tilts his head back.

"There are bags of gold coins, a goose that lays golden eggs, and a magical harp that plays the most beautiful music all by itself," I say.

"Really?" Jack asks excitedly. "Oh, wow. My mum and I could buy so much with all that gold. I can't even imagine what it would feel like to go to bed without my stomach growling. I'm always hungry."

I feel so bad for Jack and his nice mum! Hungry, tattered clothes, falling-apart chairs. The more I think about what it would be like to go to bed hungry, the more I know I did the right thing by trading Prince. For a night, anyway.

"What's the first thing you'll eat with your riches?" Jonah asks Jack.

"Definitely the fish and chips from the market. Smells so good!" Jack answers. "With extra vinegar. And for dinner, bangers and mash from The White Duck and the Black Horse. I've never eaten in a restaurant before. Well, not since my dad died when I was little."

Aww, poor Jack.

"What are bangers?" Jonah asks. "Would I like them? And what's mash?"

"If you like sausage," Jack explains, "you'll like bangers — that's what they are! And mash is just our shortened way of saying mashed potatoes."

Jonah grins. "I LOVE mashed potatoes!"

Jack high-fives Jonah. "Well, the two of us will have a proper sit-down meal once we have our gold coins."

Uh, what about me? Feeling a little left out here!

"And you too, of course, Abby," Jack says sheepishly, reading my mind.

"Yeah, Abby, you can come, too," Jonah says, beaming at Jack.

Gee, thanks, Jonah.

"So let's go get your riches!" Jonah says, leaping onto the beanstalk. He grabs ahold of a side sprout and propels himself up. "I'm a really good climber," he adds, glancing back at us.

"The higher the funner!" Jack says with a grin. "'Funner' might not be a word, but it should be!"

Jonah cracks up laughing. "You're so funny, Jack! Isn't he so funny, Abby?" Jonah calls down. He puts one hand on his belly and guffaws.

Jonah used to think I was funny. And I *am* funny! I try to think of a good joke about beanstalks or climbing, but I can't think of anything. It's hard to be funny on command.

"Jonah, two hands on the side stalks, please!" Jack calls up. "For safety!"

I frown. That's MY line. I'm the one who watches out for Jonah.

"'Kay!" Jonah calls back, carefully putting both hands on the side stalks.

"Ready, Abby?" Jack asks me. "Just put your foot on that bottom sprout and — "

"I've got this," I say quickly.

"I'm sure you do," he says. He gives me a supportive smile and a wink.

Ugh. Can't I just be annoyed at Jack in peace without him doing something cute?

I walk over to the stalk and gingerly put one foot on the bottom sprout. Do I really have to climb up ahead of Jack? First of all, I hate climbing. Second of all, I'll probably make weird huffing noises like I do in gym. Third of all —

I'm kind of scared!

But there's no way I want Jack to know that.

"Abby's a little scared of heights!" Jonah calls down. "Good thing you're here in case she falls!"

Oh, thanks again, *Jonah*!

"I won't let you fall, Abby," Jack says kindly.

"I am not going to fall," I say, my voice firm.

I adjust my foot on a bottom sprout, then grab a top

sprout and press down with my foot. Seems pretty sturdy. Well, here goes. I start climbing.

Huh. It's really not that hard since there are so many places to grab on to and for my feet to go. It's actually almost fun.

If you don't look down.

Do not look down. Do. Not. Look. Down.

Even if cute Jack is below me.

Especially because cute Jack is right below me, climbing up effortlessly. The last thing I want to do is get distracted by him and SLIP RIGHT OFF THE BEANSTALK!

"WOW!" Jonah calls from way up high. "I can see all of Tradetown from up here! There's the market," he adds, pointing.

DO NOT LOOK DOWN, I warn myself. You will freak out. Just keep looking up and make sure your feet are steady.

A cloud brushes past, and I can only see parts of Jonah up ahead. I see one of his sneakers, then it disappears as he gets higher.

A cloud? How high are we, anyway?

"Hey, guys?" Jack calls up from below me. "How do we know where all that treasure is? Is it on some cloud?"

"No, it's in the castle," Jonah shouts down.

"What castle?" I hear Jack ask.

"The one the giant man and his giant wife live in," Jonah yells down.

"Oh. *That* castle," Jack says. "Please tell me you're kidding!"

Oh, boy. Oh, no. How could I have been so thoughtless?

The giant killed Jack's dad! We should have told him we were going to THAT giant's castle.

"I mean, I know there's no such things as giants," Jack says with a laugh. "You two crack me up," he adds.

Now I'm confused. No such thing as giants?

Oh. Right. Jack doesn't know the giant killed his father! That's what the *fairy* tells Jack.

I wonder when we'll meet her.

I hope she'll be sparkly.

"Jonah, when you get to the top," Jack calls up to him, "stay behind a cloud. Don't rush in until we make a plan!"

"Good idea!" Jonah shouts down to him. He sticks out his arm and gives Jack a thumbs-up.

Before I can even tell Jonah to hold on with BOTH hands, Jack shouts it up for me.

"Oh, yeah! Thanks for looking out for me, Jack!" Jonah calls, grabbing on to a side sprout.

HUMPH. Jack is coming up with all the ideas AND watching out for MY little brother? I'm not sure I like this. I mean, I complain about having to do both all the time, but still! It's my thing!

"Everything okay, Abby?" Jack asks me.

I realize I've stopped climbing. "All good!" I say, and propel myself up.

Up and up and up I climb through the clouds — which are getting smaller and fluffier. I let myself take one peek down with one eye open.

Below me, I can just make out Jack's little wood house and the fence and barn, but they're getting smaller and smaller. I can see the town and the stone buildings and cobblestone alleyways and the market. But I'm soon above a cloud and suddenly clouds are all I can see below me. Clouds, and the top of Jack's head as he climbs up.

Another cloud floats past me. Except this cloud is . . . bright pink. I look up into the blue sky and there's an orange cloud. I look to my left and — oh, wow. The clouds up here are every color of the rainbow! Apple-green, every shade of blue, bright red, and lemon-yellow. And now a purple one floats by.

"Hey, guys," Jonah calls down. "The clouds are all different colors!"

"I see!" I say as a striped red-and-white cloud moves past the beanstalk. Another cloud has black and white polka dots.

"Awesome!" Jack says. "I've never seen anything like this before!"

I get to the top and gasp. The clouds up here are not only all different colors, but some are in the shape of animals. There's a cat. And a giraffe. And even a llama.

As the cloud animals float by us, a castle appears up ahead. It rests on a giant white cloud — and unless I'm seeing things, the castle is MADE OUT OF CLOUDS. Fluffy, puffy, cream-colored clouds instead of stone or whatever else castles are usually made of!

It's a small castle as far as castles go but incredibly TALL. It must be at least one hundred feet high. It's definitely a castle for giants.

"Wow!" Jack says, staring at it. "There really is a castle. And it's ENORMOUS!"

"There's a reason for that," I say.

"A good reason!" Jonah says. "Giants live here!"

"Come on," Jack says. "There's no such thing! Sure, I've heard people tell stories about giants, but everyone knows they're just make-believe."

"Actually, they're not," I say. "A giant really does live here. Two, actually."

"I'll believe it when I see it," Jack says as a blue-and-green-striped cloud floats past him.

Boy, is he going to be surprised.

For a few seconds, we all just stare at the puffy, wispy, yet sturdy-looking cloud castle in awe. How is it even standing?

"Just in case there IS a giant," Jack says, "I'd better think of a plan about getting into the castle. Give me a few seconds."

"Sure, Jack," Jonah says, beaming at him. "I bet your plan will be amazing."

I cross my arms over my chest. "I'VE already got a plan," I say.

"You do?" Jack asks.

"Yes. I was thinking of one the whole way up." When I wasn't worried about falling and turning into Abby mash on the ground.

"Maybe we should hear Jack's plan first," Jonah says.

"He hasn't even thought of one," I say with an edge.

"I'd like to hear Abby's idea," Jack says.

Right answer, kid.

"Yeah, me too," Jonah says, smiling at Jack.

I give Jonah the side-eye.

"Okay, guys," I say. "Here's what should happen. If we knock on the door, the giant's wife will probably answer."

"The giant has a wife?" Jack asks, looking at us in shock.

"Yes," I say. "I don't know her name, but she's supposed to be nice."

"A nice giant is a good thing," Jonah adds with a nod.

Very true. "But whatever you do," I caution, "do not let her husband see you! In fact, if the husband answers the door, run! When the wife goes into another room, we'll each take something and run out. Like the coins or the harp or the goose."

"Wait," Jack says. "We're stealing from a nice giant lady?"

Uh, when he puts it that way, I kind of realize that that is exactly what we're about to do.

"Here's the thing," I say to Jack. "The giant's wife may be nice. But the giant? NOT SO NICE. He's the opposite of nice."

"Ah. Got it," Jack says.

"So if we take a bag of gold coins," I say, "we're really just taking what he stole from someone else. That's what I heard, anyway."

It's true.

"Makes sense to me," Jack says. "And the most important thing is getting five coins to pay back that trader for your dog."

He's exactly right.

And how amazing is it that even though he's about to get really rich, he's still thinking about Prince? So amazing.

"You're so right, Jack," Jonah says. "The most important thing is getting Prince back."

Even though I just thought the same thing, I roll my eyes. I hate that I'm feeling . . . kind of jealous. My brother is treating Jack the way he used to treat me. Like the one who knows everything. I like being the one who knows everything! But Jack *does* know a lot of stuff, too.

Is it possible to have a crush on someone and feel jealous of them at the same time?

This is so confusing.

"Then let's go," Jack says, marching up the cloud walkway between the beanstalk and the castle.

The walkway is not exactly what I'm used to. It's made out of fluffy green clouds that look like grass, and is lined with cloud flowers of every color.

Finally, we make it to the front door of the castle. It's arched and made out of blue clouds that look like marshmallows stuck together. I reach out a hand to touch the door to see if it'll feel like cotton or marshmallows, but the door feels like wood.

Strange.

I knock on the door. It barely makes a sound. "Guys, help me!" I say to Jonah and Jack. "We have to be loud."

We all hit the door again and again. Finally, the door opens. I see a pair of shoes at my eye level. They are not made out of clouds — they're just normal shoes. Purple velvet slippers, actually.

We all look up. Way up. Way, way, WAY up.

The giant's wife is standing there. She's at least fifty feet tall. She's wearing a long silver skirt and a multicolored sweater. As far as I can tell, her clothes aren't made out of clouds. She has a long gray braid down one shoulder, brown skin, round cheeks, and big brown eyes.

"Well, hullo down there," she says. "Lovely day, isn't it?"

"Yes!" I say. "For once it's not all misty and drizzly."

"We're above the clouds," the giant's wife says. "The weather changes moment to moment. I'm Philippa."

"I'm Abby, this is my brother, Jonah, and that's our friend Jack." I curtsy. It seems like the right thing to do.

"Wow, you really ARE a giant!" Jack says. He curtsies, too.

Philippa beams. "There aren't many of us," she explains. "Just a hundred left across giantdoms in the skies. But yes, we do exist."

"Wow," Jack says again.

Jonah curtsies just like Jack did.

"Aren't you darling?" Philippa exclaims, her enormous hand coming down toward Jonah's head.

My brother's eyes widen.

Uh-oh.

Thankfully, Philippa gives him a very gentle pat with her pinkie. Whew. She smiles at all of us.

"I thought I was gonna be a pancake," Jonah whispers to me.

"I'm glad you're not," I whisper back.

"Well, come in, the three of you," she says. "I love having some company since my husband sleeps half the day away. But be quiet. You don't want to wake a sleeping giant."

No, we don't.

She pulls the door open wide. We walk into a hallway and follow Philippa into the kitchen. Nothing inside the castle seems to be made of clouds. There's a wooden table the size of our school's soccer field. And the chairs are like ten couches put together.

"I just made some vanilla scones if you're hungry," Philippa says.

“I’d love a scone,” I say — because I would, AND we need to buy some time. While Philippa is getting the scones, we can look for the bags of gold coins. I wonder if we’ll see the goose that lays the golden eggs and the magical harp.

“Oh, where are my manners?” Philippa says. “You probably want to sit down for a bit. My husband is in the process of building a dollhouse for his little niece in another giantdom. I’ll just go get the kitchen set from that. The table and chairs will be just the right size for you three. Stay put, dears. Back in a jiff.”

She leaves the room, the thudding of her feet booming in our ears.

“Wow, she’s super nice,” I say.

“Very,” Jonah agrees.

And the giant is building a dollhouse for his niece? How sweet!

“I sure would love a scone,” Jack says, rubbing his stomach. “My mum likes to bake, but we never have enough flour or eggs for biscuits or cakes.”

That’s sure going to change.

Which reminds me. We need to look for the coins while Philippa is out of the room and the giant is asleep.

"Do you see big bags that might be full of coins anywhere?" I ask, looking all around the kitchen. The problem is that I can barely see on TOP of anything. We're teensy in the giant's house.

Jack climbs one of the chair legs and hangs on to the side like a pirate on a ship. He looks around. "I don't see any bags."

"Maybe they keep the gold coins in the living room," I suggest. "Quick, let's look."

But before I can even turn around, I hear a really weird sound. A sniffing sound. Like someone is smelling the air.

SNIFF. SNIFF-SNIFF.

I look at Jonah and Jack.

THUD. THUD-THUD-THUD.

Oh, no.

"What's that noise?" Jonah asks, covering his ears.

"I've never even heard thunder that loud!" Jack says.

THUD-THUD-THUD.

It sounds like Philippa's heavy footsteps, only much, much louder.

What could it be?

THUD-THUD-THUD.

The sound is coming closer!

"Fee, fi, fo, fum," booms a very loud man's voice. "I smell the blood of an Englishman!"

Crumbs.

I guess we woke the sleeping giant.

chapter eight

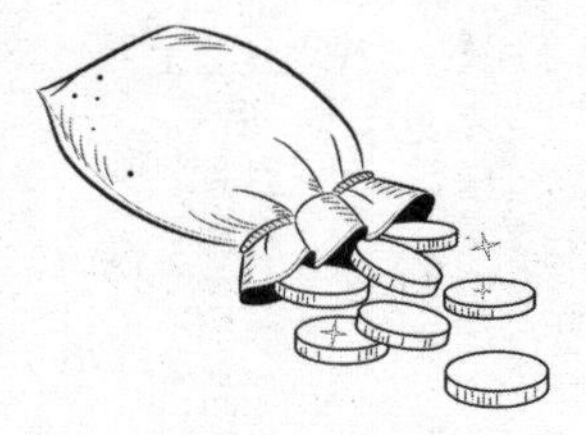

Fee, Fi, Oh, No

"Hide!" I cry.

We can't get caught by the giant. He eats kids for snacks! Plus, he's a murderer! He killed Jack's dad!

"Where should we go?" Jack asks.

"In the story, Jack hides in the oven," Jonah says, pointing up at the oven.

"What story?" Jack asks, but there's no time to answer him now.

"The oven is too risky!" I say. "Also too hot. Philippa just made scones."

And I'm not even sure we could reach the oven.

In the corner of the kitchen, I spot a tall, narrow door with slats. It's slightly ajar, so I peek in. It's a pantry full of giant-sized cans and jars and boxes of food. The giants sure like pasta. And sour cream and onion potato chips.

"In here!" I whisper.

Jack and Jonah race in after me, and I shut the door. We can just see through the slats into the kitchen.

THUD-THUD-THUD.

The thudding gets louder and louder until finally the giant enters the kitchen.

I can't see all of him through the slats. But I can see part of his gray pants. They're huge.

And so is he.

"Fee, fi, fo, fum!" the giant sings. "I smell the blood of an Englishman. Be he alive or be he dead, I'll grind his bones to make my bread!"

Jonah, Jack, and I all gulp at the same time.

"I guess THAT'S how the rest of the song goes," Jonah whispers, his eyes wide.

The giant's bread is made from bones? That is disgusting.

There are so many kinds of bread. Sourdough bread. Challah bread. But kid bread?

AHHHH!

I press my face up against the slats so I can get a better view.

"Oh, Magnus," Philippa scolds, following her husband into the kitchen. "Please don't sing that song. It's so gruesome." She looks around the kitchen, clearly trying to see what happened to us.

The giant laughs. The sound reverberates through the house. "But my dad taught it to me. And I think it's funny!"

"It's not," Philippa says.

The giant looks around the kitchen, sniffing the air.

"Philippa!" Magnus says.

"Yes, dear?" she asks.

I hear the sniffing again.

"I really do smell a boy," Magnus says. "Or two boys. And maybe a girl? I smell a lot of small people."

Jonah, Jack, and I all remain frozen, holding our breaths.

"I don't know what to tell you, Magnus," Philippa says. "I don't smell anyone."

Thank you, Philippa! She's covering for us. Whew. Or maybe she just thinks we left.

Magnus shrugs. "I'd love one of your delicious vanilla scones and some tea, dear."

"Coming right up, sweetie," Philippa says.

The giant walks over to a kitchen cabinet that's right above the counter and opens it.

I gasp. Inside is an open burlap sack stuffed with huge gold coins!

"The coins!" I whisper to Jonah and Jack.

Jack smiles. "Thanks, Magnus," he whispers. "Now we know where they are."

I spot many more burlap sacks, each tied with a red ribbon at the top, behind the one sack the giant is now holding. The bags are massive. Will we be able to grab one and carry it out? "I'll count my coins until my snack is ready," Magnus says, grabbing the sack and sitting down at the table with a thud.

Your coins? Ha! He stole Jack's dad's money and probably a ton of other people's, too. No wonder he got so rich!

I watch Magnus take out a big gold coin and examine it. "One," he says, putting it aside. He takes out another.

"Two." And another. "Three." By the time he counts out twenty-two gold coins, his head is rolled back and he's snoring. Who knew counting coins was as boring as counting sheep?

Have you ever heard a train rumble right past you? That's kind of what giant snores sound like.

Through the slats, I watch Philippa walk over to Magnus. He lets out a super-rumbly snore. "I suppose your scone can wait," she whispers with a chuckle. She takes the bag of coins and stashes it back in the cabinet. "Kids?" she calls softly, looking around. "Are you still here?"

I put my finger to my lips, motioning to Jack and Jonah to be quiet.

She shrugs. "I guess they left. I think I'll go put my feet up in the living room. See what's on the telly."

Philippa thuds out of the room. Her footfalls aren't as loud as Magnus's but they're still LOUD.

"This is our chance," I whisper to Jonah and Jack. "Let's grab as many coins as we can carry from the cabinet and get out of here!"

"Wait. What about the goose that lays the golden eggs?" Jonah asks. "Shouldn't we look for that, too?"

"Oh!" Jack says, his eyes lighting up. "A goose that can lay golden eggs will mean we'll never go hungry again. And my mum could buy me a new coat for winter. I outgrew mine. And gloves to keep my hands warm. And maybe a cap to keep the rain off my head. A boy can dream, right?"

Poor Jack. He deserves all those necessities! And more! But I don't see a goose. Or the harp. And do we really want to RISK becoming kid bread for the giant's next ham-and-cheese sandwich?

"I think it's too dangerous," I say. "The goose could be in another part of the castle, and by the time we find her, Magnus could wake up."

"Come on, Abby!" Jonah whispers. "Jack needs the goose now!"

I stare at Jack's tattered shirt and the holes in the knees of his pants. I think about how little he and his mother have. Gold coins can't last forever. But a goose that lays golden eggs means real wealth. It means a new coat every year if Jack needs it. And Jack and his mom are so kind . . .

Outside the pantry, the giant lets out a long, loud snore. Jonah, Jack, and I glance at each other.

"Never mind. Forget the goose. It's way too risky," Jack says. "Let's get the coins and go."

"Jack's right," Jonah agrees. "Magnus might wake up and catch us. I don't want to be kid bread. Good thing you're here, Jack!"

Really? Didn't I just say that a second ago?

"Okay," I say, determined to take back my rightful place as Planner. "I'm going to open the pantry door very quietly but quickly. Then we just have to get to the cabinet and grab a bag of coins."

"Let's do it!" Jack agrees.

I push open the pantry door, hoping it won't squeak like ours does at home. No squeak! Phew. We all tiptoe out. Magnus is snoring so loudly the whole kitchen shakes.

I immediately see a problem. The cabinet with the gold coins is above the counter.

"How exactly are we getting UP to the cabinet?" I ask. For us, it's like getting up to the roof of a house from the ground.

Think of something good before Jack does, I tell myself. Think, think!

I stare at the cabinet. Then the counter below it. Then the bottom row of cabinets. Hmmm. Maybe?

"We can climb up the bottom cabinet," I suggest. "See the handle? We each just need a running leap to grab the handle and fling ourselves up onto the counter. Then we'll do the same with the top cabinet."

"I don't know," Jack says. "It sounds dangerous. And how would we get the huge, heavy bag of coins out of the cabinet and out of the castle and down the beanstalk? Did you see the size of those coins?"

I cluck my tongue in annoyance. "One thing at a time, Jack. I'm getting us up to the cabinet! Then we'll worry about next steps."

"But Jack's right," Jonah says. "I think he should come up with a different idea."

Of course Jonah would side with Jack.

"I guess we could try Abby's plan," Jack says, "and then worry about each next thing as we get to it."

"GREAT idea!" Jonah says, holding up his palm for a high five.

Seriously?

"Although," Jack adds, rubbing his chin, "we do need a lookout and someone to direct us from the ground."

"I'll be the lookout," I volunteer. This way I don't have to climb. From my position, I can see the giant sleeping AND the cabinet where the gold coins are.

I watch Jonah and Jack follow my plan. They get a running start and grab on to the handles of the lower cabinet to hoist themselves up. Then Jonah puts his foot on the handle and grasps the top of the counter. He flings himself up and on top. Jack does the same. Then Jack turns and gives me a thumbs-up sign.

"Hurry!" I whisper-yell. I turn around and look at the giant. He's still sleeping.

Jack and Jonah run to the middle cabinet.

"I can't reach the cabinet!" Jonah whispers, jumping up and trying to reach the handle. "Now what?"

"Wait," Jack says, eyeing the distance. "I think I can!" He stands on his tiptoes and tries to open the door but can't reach. "Just a bit higher," he squeaks, stretching himself even taller. He reaches! He's able to get the door open!

"Thank goodness my mum got me these new sneakers!"

Jack says with a grin. "I'm a good two centimeters taller in these. My old ones were completely flattened."

I have no idea how to convert centimeters into inches. But yay, Jack's mum!

I like the word *mum.* I wonder if I should start calling my mom "Mum." Or "Mummy."

That kind of makes me think she should be wrapped in toilet paper and coming back from the dead. Never mind.

"But I don't think I can get to the sack," Jack is saying. "It's too far inside."

I look over. It's true. Jack needs to be at least a FOOT taller to reach inside the cabinet for the sack of coins.

"I know," I say. "Jack, let Jonah sit on your shoulders. He can climb into the cabinet and push out the sack."

"Not a bad idea!" Jack says. "Let's do it!"

"Not a bad idea at all!" Jonah repeats.

Jack kneels down, and Jonah climbs onto his shoulders.

Here we go.

"SNOOOOOOOORT!" goes the giant.

We all freeze.

We wait a moment, but the giant doesn't move.

"Keep going," I say.

"But be careful," Jack says.

AGAIN — that's MY line.

"I will!" Jonah promises.

I watch as Jonah leaps from Jack's shoulders and right into the cabinet. Yes!

"I'm gonna push out the sack," Jonah says. "Jack, move out of the way or it'll smush you!"

Jack races to the far side of the counter. Jonah uses all his strength to push out the burlap sack of coins. It lands with a thud on the counter.

I glance at Magnus. He's still sleeping! Yes!

"Yay!" I say. "Great job!"

Jack gives Jonah a high five. "Awesome, little dude."

"I wouldn't say I'm little," Jonah mutters, but then grins. "Maybe compared to Magnus."

Jack pushes the sack off the counter onto the floor. It lands with another heavy thud. I hold my breath and glance at the giant again. He stirs but doesn't wake up. I can hear Philippa humming to herself in another room. So far, so good.

Jonah and Jack climb down to the floor and rush back over to me. Phew.

Just then, though, Magnus stirs again with a low rumble-snore. I glance up. He's still sleeping.

But his hand drops off the table.

His super-huge, beefy, GIANT HAND. And it's headed right for where Jack is standing. The giant's hand pushes him right over like he's a bowling pin. Jack goes flying across the room.

Ahhhh!

Jonah and I race to where Jack landed on the other side of the kitchen.

"Jack! Are you okay?" Jonah asks, shaking Jack's arm desperately.

Jack rubs his back and sits up. "I'm okay," he says. "Just a little sore. Ouch. We should get out of here."

Jonah and I help Jack stand back up. We all look over at the big, heavy bag of coins on the floor.

"Uh, next problem," Jack says. "How are we gonna get the bag of coins to the door and down the beanstalk?"

Good question.

"Let's all grab part of the top and drag the bag to the door," I say. "Together."

"Team Teamwork!" Jonah says, reaching for a section of sack. Jack and I do, too.

"Ready?" I ask. We can all hear Magnus still snoring, so we know he's still asleep. But we don't know for how long. "Pull!" I say.

We all pull. The sack is really heavy. But it'll be worth the effort.

We make it all the way to the door, which, thankfully, Philippa left open. We drag the bag down the cloud walkway, all of us huffing and puffing.

"There's the beanstalk," I say when the huge, bright green top of it comes into view. "How are we going to get the sack down?" I ask.

"We could just drop it," Jonah suggests.

Jack rubs his chin. "Hmm. It'll get down before we do," he points out, "but at least we'll be sure it'll land on the ground. You know. Gravity."

"But what if someone happens to be standing in that spot?" I say. "Like your mother! She'll get hit with it."

Jack's hazel-green eyes widen. "I definitely don't want

my mum or anyone else to get hurt. Forget the gravity plan!"

We all stare at the bag of coins again.

"I have an idea!" Jack says. "How about if I slide down the beanstalk to the bottom and make sure there's no one around. Then I'll shout up for you two to drop the bag!"

"Brilliant!" Jonah says. "Yay, Jack!"

Oh. It *is* a pretty good idea.

"Okay," I say to Jack. "You slide down and tell us when. Then Jonah and I will push the bag off the cloud."

"I'm on it!" Jack says. He leaps onto the beanstalk, then shimmies right down the center.

At least getting down looks a lot more fun than climbing up.

I watch Jack go through a red-and-purple cloud, then I can't see him.

"Halfway there!" he calls up. "Almost to the ground!" I hear him call more faintly. "Okay, I'm on the ground. All clear!"

"LOOK OUT!" I shout as loud as I can.

Jonah and I push the bag off the edge of the cloud walkway and watch it fall, fall, fall through the colorful clouds.

Thud.

"All good!" Jack calls up.

"Phew!" Jonah says. He grabs a stem sticking out of the beanstalk. Gulp. "Here I goooo!" he calls, and slides down.

Now it's my turn.

I carefully grab on to a stem and start shimmying down the beanstalk.

Ooh.

This is really FUN!!!!!!

I slide down, down, down, right through the multi-colored clouds. Ooh, there's a super-fluffy pink one that looks just like cotton candy. And there's one that's half orange and half blue — the colors of Smithville Elementary. And look! This one's all sparkly!

Hmm. Sparkles. When do we meet the fairy?

A minute later, I'm back on solid ground with Jack and Jonah. Feels good.

"Hey, Jonah," I say. "When do we meet the fairy?"

"Who?" Jack asks, grabbing an old peeling red wheelbarrow from the yard. Jonah and I help him hoist the sack of coins into the wheelbarrow.

"The fairy," I say.

"The fairy riding a peacock," Jonah adds.

A peacock? "Don't fairies already fly?" I ask. "Why would she need to ride a peacock?"

Jonah shrugs.

Jack looks at us and grins. "Well, yesterday I would have said there's no such things as fairies. But now I know that magic beans exist. And beanstalks that grow into the sky. And giants! Who'd have ever thought? So I guess fairies are real, too."

"Yep," I say, thinking of all the magic Jonah and I have seen in fairy tales.

Jonah scratches his head, looking worried. "Hmm," Jonah says. "It's true, Abby. We *should* have met the fairy by now."

"Don't fret, mate," Jack says to Jonah. "Was the fairy going to help us get up to the castle or something? If so, we didn't need her. We have what we went for." He points at the sack in the wheelbarrow. "Even if we didn't get the goose and the magic harp you mentioned."

"I guess," I say.

"But the fairy is supposed to be the one to tell you all about what that awful giant did to your dad," Jonah says.

Jack tilts his head and stares at Jonah.

"He doesn't know," I say to Jonah. "Because we haven't met the fairy yet."

Jonah's face falls and his shoulders slump. "Oh, yeah." He turns to Jack. "Sorry I said something. I didn't want to be the one to tell you."

"Wait," Jack says. "What are you talking about? What awful thing did the giant do to my dad?"

"I'm sorry to be the one to . . . um, spill the beans again, but the giant killed your father," Jonah says, bowing his head.

"Huh?" Jack asks. He looks confused. "The giant didn't kill my father."

"Huh?" Jonah asks, scrunching up his face.

"Huh?" I ask.

Jack shakes his head. "My dad caught a bad illness that was going around a few years ago. He died from that. He told me he loved me and my mum with his last breath. I sure do miss my pop," he adds with a wistful sigh.

Aww.

That's so sad about Jack's dad. But if the giant didn't kill Jack's dad, then —

"Hey, Abby," Jonah whispers. "I think I know why we haven't met the fairy."

I think I know, too.

Because we're not in that version of the story.

chapter nine

Saving Prince

Which means — we're in the version of the story that *I* know.

And if the giant didn't kill Jack's dad or steal his money . . . then Magnus's gold coins belong to him and Philippa and only to them. Which makes sense. Why would Jack's dad have had giant-sized coins anyway?

So we stole the coins. From perfectly nice giants. Who were probably saving up to go on vacation or something.

Although they did want to eat us.

Maybe. They didn't actually try to eat us. One of them only sang a song about eating us. Is that just as bad?

On the plus side, in the version we're in, Jack probably doesn't marry a princess. So maybe one day . . .

Focus, Abby, focus!

"So I guess that means we're thieves," Jonah whispers to me.

"But for a good cause," I remind him. "We still need five gold coins to save Prince!"

And it's not like we can lug the sack of gold coins back *up* the beanstalk! Right?

"Let's go get Prince right now!" Jonah says.

What's clear is that neither of us wants to think too long or too hard about the situation. We have to save our dog.

I nod. I untie the top of the burlap sack. "Wow, there must be hundreds of gold coins in here!"

"And the giant had SO many more bags," Jack says. "So he surely won't miss one measly bag."

Maybe. But still.

"So should we count them and then split them three ways?" Jack asks.

"Ooh!" Jonah says excitedly, but I nudge him.

"You really are so sweet," I tell Jack. "But Jonah and I

only need five. The rest are for you." I reach in and take out five coins for Prince.

"Wow, are you sure?" Jack says. "Awesome! Thank you. I'll just wheel this wheelbarrow inside and lock it up in a closet. Be right back." He rushes the wheelbarrow into the house, then comes out again. "My mum's not home. She left a note that she's visiting a friend. I can't wait to show her the gold coins."

Jonah grins. "Now let's go untrade Prince!"

The three of us hurry along the gravel road toward town. It's afternoon, so the town is crowded with people, and the market is even more crowded. I try to remember the address and directions Devin gave us. Left turn one alley up from the biscuit stall. Two twists, three turns. House 19. Got it!

"The biscuit stall is just over there," Jack says, pointing to a booth with an elderly woman inside.

We rush to the stall. I don't see or smell biscuits, but there are tons of yummy-looking cookies.

"Where are the biscuits?" Jonah asks, looking at the trays of cookies.

Jack points at the table. "Right there. Yum, oatmeal raisin! My favorite."

"Huh?" Jonah asks. "Those are cookies. Not biscuits."

Oh, wait! "Here cookies are called biscuits," I explain. "Like soccer is called football."

"Ohhhhhhhh," Jonah says. "Well, those are the most delicious-looking biscuits I've ever seen. Can we buy some?"

I snort-laugh. He is *really* trying to impress Jack. "You want oatmeal raisin cookies? Seriously? You hate cookies with raisins! And anyway, I have EXACTLY five gold coins on me. Which we need to get Prince back."

"Right! Forget the cookie-biscuits," Jonah exclaims, his cheeks turning red.

I glance to the left. There's the correct alleyway.

"Let's go!" Jack says. "Number nineteen will be around the curve, to the right, to the left again, then three more right curves."

He leads the way down the cobblestone alley. I would not want to ride my bike on this road. Way too bumpy. The houses are very narrow and made of black stone. The street curves and curves, and finally, there is number 19! Hurrah!

I just hope Prince is here, and that he's okay. I take a deep breath, and run up to the door and knock.

Ruff! Ruff-ruff.

I hear Prince!

Phew.

The trader opens the door a crack. I can see a gold chain keeping the door latched. I expect Prince to come rushing out to us. But I don't see him.

"Hi, we have your gold coins," I tell Devin. "Where's Prince?"

"Sorry," Devin says, "but I changed my mind about the trade."

EXQUEEZE ME?

"You . . . you . . . can't do that!" I shout.

"I just did!" Devin snaps. "I love animals and want to keep Prince. So if you want him back, you'll need to trade a different animal for him."

"No fair!" Jonah yelps.

"Yeah! A deal is a deal!" Jack adds.

The trader shrugs. "I didn't sign a contract, so . . ."

I knew it, I knew it, I knew it.

"Do you want your dog back or not?" Devin asks.

"Of course we do!" I say, glaring at him.

"Fine. Then trade me another animal for him. But not just ANY old animal."

"Huh?" Jonah asks.

"I want the goose that lays the golden eggs," Devin says, his eyes gleaming.

Jack's mouth drops open.

I glare at Devin. "How do YOU know about that goose?"

"All giants have geese as pets," he says. "Duh."

There's no way that's true. "How did you even know about the giant in the first place?" I ask, folding my arms across my chest.

"Stop asking so many questions!" Devin says. "I have a headache."

"You deserve a headache," Jack snaps. "You're not being fair to Abby and Jonah."

"Yeah!" Jonah agrees with a frown.

Devin sighs. "Sorry, children. But sometimes deals change. Like NOW."

"This is SO wrong!" I say.

"Tough. The goose for the dog!" Devin says, then slams the door in our faces.

Which means we have to go back to the giant's castle. And Magnus is probably pretty upset that a bag of his coins went missing.

A sleeping giant I can deal with. I'm not so sure about an angry one.

chapter ten

Giants Are People, Too

It's getting dark, so we decide not to climb up the beanstalk tonight. We'll have to wait until morning. Which means another night without Prince.

I miss him so much. His little paws. His soft fur. His cute little face. I can't believe we traded him! What were we thinking?

Luckily, we're still okay on time. We have to get home by noon tomorrow. But we can do that. It's tight, but we can do it.

Hopefully.

When we get to Jack's house, Ada comes running outside to ask Jack why there's a giant beanstalk in the yard. He tells her everything — well, he leaves out the part about the giants' castle. He just says that we climbed up the beanstalk and found a bag of gold coins waiting up top. I mean, that's *sort* of true. I can tell Jack feels bad about lying to his mom — er, mum — but it's probably smart not to tell her about the giants. She'd be pretty worried about that, and then she definitely wouldn't want us going *back* up there.

We go inside the house and Jack shows his mom the sack of gold coins in the wheelbarrow.

"Wow!" Ada says. "Thank goodness you kids got those magic beans, after all! Sorry I doubted you, Jackie." She gives him a big hug.

I could use a hug. A Prince hug. Boo.

"Well, look around, kids," Ada says. "This is the last time you'll see any of these shabby furnishings! We can even move to a nice new house, Jack," she adds. "You'll have a proper bedroom!"

As Jack and his mom talk about all the things they'll finally be able to buy and all the meals they can't wait to eat,

Jonah and I get into bed. I want tomorrow to come fast so that I can get the goose, give him to Devin, and get my dog back.

We're coming, Prince!

The next morning, we wake up at 6:00 A.M., which is also 6:00 A.M. in Smithville. Good thing every hour at home is seven hours here, or we'd be in trouble!

Jack's mom makes us small bowls of porridge and then we head back outside to the beanstalk. We told Ada we were climbing up again today to check and see if there were other gold coins to be found.

Like last time, Jonah climbs up first. Then I do.

"Good job, Abby!" Jack calls up to me from below.

I smile down at him. He smiles back.

Focus on the mission, Abby. Not the boy!

So back up I go. Up, up, up.

When I start to see the different-colored clouds, I know we're getting close to the top.

Once all three of us make it up to the top, we go running down the cloud walkway to the castle. Then we pause at the front door.

"What now?" I whisper.

No way am I knocking on the door this time. Philippa probably knows we took the coins. She won't be happy to see us. And forget about Magnus . . .

"I hear voices," Jonah says. "Coming from around the side of the castle."

"Shhh!" I say, holding a finger to my lips. "Let's go see."

I tiptoe to the end of the house, Jack and Jonah right behind me. We all peer around the side.

The two giants are in the garden. They're both kneeling down in the clouds and pruning rosebushes.

"Smell those beautiful rose petals!" Philippa says, breathing in the scent.

Magnus sniffs and we can hear it all the way from where we're crouching.

Oops. I sure hope he doesn't smell US.

"They smell wonderful," he says. "And they're beautiful like you," he adds, giving Philippa a kiss on the cheek.

"Oh, you!" she says with a big smile. "Such a romantic."

Um, are the giants being sweet? My parents get all lovey-dovey like that sometimes and I pretend it makes me ill, but really? I kind of love it.

"Aww, they're cute," Jack says. "Surprisingly so."

"Right?" I say. Then I remember why we're here. To be goose-nappers. "Ugh, I hate that we're stealing from them. They don't deserve this."

We watch as Magnus plucks a flower and slips it into Philippa's hair. Then he gives her another kiss on the cheek and they rub their giant noses together.

"We're doing it to get Prince back," Jack reminds me. "Sometimes, you have to do something wrong to make up for something wrong. Know what I mean?"

"I think I do," Jonah says.

Me too. Jack is right. Besides, we have no choice.

We rush back to the front door. The giants must have left it open when they came outside. They are really bad with safety. It's like they're asking for us to rob them!

In the kitchen, I listen for goose sounds, but then realize I have no idea what sounds a goose makes. Like a duck? I definitely don't hear quacking. Or anything, really.

"Let's try the bedroom," Jack suggests.

We go down the hallway and sneak into the giants' bedroom. They have an enormous bed the size of an Olympic swimming pool. Above the bed is a huge photograph in a gold frame of Magnus and Philippa on the dance floor, Philippa in a wedding gown and Magnus in a tux. One wall of the bedroom is full of massively tall bookcases stuffed with books. In front of the window is an easel with a big canvas on it and paintbrushes in a bucket beneath it. Someone has been painting the multicolored clouds outside.

Magnus and Philippa seem like such nice, regular giants. Besides the eating-children part.

"No goose in here," Jack says, looking around. "Let's try the living room."

"Or maybe the goose has her OWN room," Jonah says. "She does lay golden eggs, after all. She certainly deserves her own mansion, never mind her own room."

"Smart thinking," Jack says, winking at Jonah.

Jonah's whole face lights up.

"I'll check the other bedrooms," Jack says. "You guys check the living room."

As the three of us leave the bedroom, I look at the photographs lining the walls of the hallway. Magnus and Philippa doing things together: out to dinner, walking in a park, floating on a cloud.

I frown. We shouldn't be here. We shouldn't be walking into their home and taking their stuff.

It's wrong.

Plain and simple.

"Guys?" I say, turning to Jack and Jonah. They stop and look at me.

"What is it?" Jack asks me.

"This isn't right," I say, feeling choked up. "Even if Magnus eats children for snacks. It's his house! And we're in it! Eating kids for a giant is like us eating chicken fingers!"

"Chicken fingers aren't really fingers of chicken, you know," Jonah says.

"Yes, Jonah, I know that. But chickens are still animals. Just like we are to the giant. We wouldn't want someone stealing from us just because we eat animals."

Jonah frowns. "We wouldn't want chickens stealing from us?"

"You know what I mean!"

"I know what you mean," Jack says. "But do you want your dog back or not?"

"Of course!" I snap. "But it's still wrong. Magnus has nothing to do with Devin and Prince."

"Well, the giant has the goose," Jack reminds me. "And Devin WANTS the goose. Therefore, we're here to get the goose. Just try to keep your focus on the most important thing."

Which is . . . Prince.

Ugh. I hate what I'm about to do.

"Fine, let's just get the goose and go!" I say. But I don't feel good about any of this. Also is the goose going to be giant-sized? If so, how will we smuggle her out of the house?

Jack goes into one of the other bedrooms, then comes out and shakes his head. "No goose in there." He goes into the next room. "Or in there."

We all go into the living room. I don't see anything goose-ish, like a goose bed or goose food. Not that I know what geese eat. Bread? Fish?

And I don't see any golden eggs.

"Where could that goose be?" I ask.

THUD. THUD-THUD.

Uh-oh.

The thudding footsteps stop.

"Fee, fi, fo, fum," Magnus chants. "I smell the blood of an Englishman. Be he alive or be he dead, I'll grind his bones to make my bread."

THUD. THUD-THUD.

Ahhh! The giant is coming!

And we didn't find the goose!

"Abby!" Jonah cries. "Is that the harp?"

I look where he's pointing. Yes! A golden harp is on a stand in the corner of the living room. The harp is massive. Three times the size of me.

Jack rushes over and puts the harp on his back. "Let's go! Before the giant gets us."

"How are you holding that?" I ask. "You're going to hurt yourself!"

"It's surprisingly light!" Jack says. "Come on!"

"But we can't leave without the goose," I say. "Or Devin won't give us Prince."

"Devin will probably want the harp," Jack assures me. "It's gold!"

"And it sings on demand," Jonah reminds me.

"Even better!" Jack says. "Cool. Devin will definitely want it, then."

THUD-THUD-THUD.

"Fee, fi, fo, fum," the giant begins.

"Oh, not that again," Philippa scolds.

"I knew I smelled children the other day!" Magnus says in his booming voice.

I hear a cabinet in the kitchen opening and shutting. UH-OH.

"And I was right," Magnus says. "Because someone stole a bag of my gold coins. They must be back. Search the house!"

Ahhh!

"We have to hide!" I hiss to Jack and Jonah.

We go racing behind the huge couch. It's the size of ten SUVs stacked on top of each other and at least twenty SUVs long.

THUD-THUD-THUD.

Magnus is coming!

"Abby, Jonah," Jack says. "The minute Magnus comes in, sneak along the back of the couch to the doorway, then run out. We're so little compared to him that he won't see us."

"Okay!" I say. It's a good plan. Even I have to admit that.

SNIFF. SNIFF-SNIFF.

"FEE, FI — " Magnus begins. "Oh, wait, I already said that," he adds.

I peek around the couch. Magnus is stepping farther into the room. Jack, Jonah, and I scoot to the far side of the couch.

"Now!" Jack whispers. "Run!"

Jonah and I hurry behind him, trying to help him hold up the massive harp. Which is *not* as light as Jack said it was!

We all go racing out into the living room, and into the kitchen. We make it and hide behind a broom that's leaning against the wall.

SNIFF-SNIFF-SNIFF!

"Philly!" Magnus calls. "Am I losing my mind? I swear I smell children. But I don't see them anywhere."

"Oh, they probably left already," Philippa responds. Her voice is coming from the bedroom, which means the coast is clear. "Don't get yourself all worked up, honey bunny."

Honey bunny? Really?

"Let's rush out of the house now," I whisper to Jonah and Jack.

I take one more look at Honey Bunny — aka the giant. He throws his hands up in the air and looks upset, but at least he's not coming after us.

Jack slings the harp over his shoulder, and then the three of us go rushing out the front door and down the cloud walkway.

"I sure hope the trader wants the harp," Jonah says as Jack jumps onto the beanstalk and slides right down.

Jonah follows, and I slide down right after him.

Finally, we reach the ground. Yes!

We go running to the market, but after the first hill, I have to take a break. Jack, holding the harp, is sweating. Jonah is raring to go.

After a few minutes' rest, we run to the trader's house. The harp is *not* light. We are all sweating.

Totally out of breath, I knock on the trader's door.

Ruff! Prince barks. *Ruff-ruff!*

"Prince," I call, my heart leaping at the sound of him. "We're here! We're going to take you home."

The door opens. The gold chain is up again and keeps the door open just an inch. I can see Devin's brown eyes and his nose and part of his mouth.

"Do you have the goose that lays the golden eggs?" Devin says.

I bite my lip. "Uh, here's the thing. We couldn't find the goose anywhere. But we did find this!" I say, pointing at the harp in Jack's arms.

"A harp?" Devin asks with a scowl. "Why do I want a harp? I'm not musical. I can't even carry a tune."

"The harp does the work for you," I explain. "It's a gold magic harp that plays beautifully on command."

Devin raises an eyebrow. "Let's hear it."

"Harp," I say, "Play 'Twinkle, Twinkle, Little Star.'"

The harp begins to play all by itself. The melody is so beautiful that Devin's eyes get misty with tears.

"I love that song," he says, dabbing under his eyes. "That was just lovely, Harp. Thank you."

The harp plays a note as if saying, *You're welcome!*

Devin's eyes gleam. He looks very pleased.

Yes! He's going to accept the trade!

"But it's not the goose," Devin says, turning away. "No goose, no Prince!" he shouts, shutting the door in our faces. Again.

chapter eleven

Third Time's the Charm

"Abby, Jonah, don't take this the wrong way," Jack begins, wiping the sweat from his forehead. "But you COULD always adopt another dog. Right?"

I stop in the middle of the cobblestone street and practically bump into the harp, which we're all still carrying.

"I do take that the wrong way," I say. "Prince is not just a random dog. He's part of our family."

"Yeah, Jack," Jonah says with a frown. He looks pretty disappointed that his hero would even suggest such a thing.

"I'm just being practical, I guess," Jack says with a shrug. "We couldn't find the goose. And the giants are onto us. We probably shouldn't go back up to their castle. So you might have to accept that Prince now belongs to Devin. I'm really sorry, guys."

"Prince belongs to US!" I cry. "So of course we're going back! We have to find that goose!"

Jack leans the harp against the side of another house and folds his arms over his chest. "I wouldn't if I were you. Because here's what's going to happen if you go back."

I fold my arms over my chest, too, and wait.

"The giants will sniff you out in a second," Jack insists. "And this time, they'll catch you."

"We'll be very careful," I say.

"Sure," Jack says. "But while you're being careful and finding the goose and running out with it, guess who might not be so lucky?" He points at Jonah. "Your little brother. He'll probably get caught. Jonah's a great kid. You want his bones ground up for the giant's toast?"

"Of course not!" I snap. How *dare* Jack suggest that? And to think I thought he was cute. Hmmpf!

"Abby would never let that happen!" Jonah says.

"Thanks, Jonah," I say, feeling slightly better.

Then Jonah looks sheepishly at Jack. "Do you really think I'm a great kid?"

"Sure do," Jack says, giving Jonah a high five. "I'm just trying to look out for you."

Oh, brother.

"So do you guys agree, then?" Jack asks me and Jonah. "No going back up the beanstalk? It's not safe!"

He looks so sincere. Ugh. I get it. I really do. BUT STILL. This is Prince he's talking about. And Prince is not his dog. So of course Jack doesn't care about him the way we do.

"Jonah?" I say. "What do you think?"

I'm terrified he'll say that Jack is right, and we shouldn't take the risk of going back just so we can rescue Prince.

But then, to my relief, Jonah shakes his head. "We need to get Prince," he says. "We can't go home without him!"

"Exactly," I say. I turn to Jack. "We're going back to get that goose and save our dog," I say. "With or without you. Come on, Jonah."

Jonah and I take off running back to Jack's house.

"Wait!" I hear.

I stop and turn around.

"I'll help you look for the goose," Jack says, jogging up behind us and carrying the harp. "Even though I think you're making a mistake. But can you help *me* carry the harp back?"

The three of us carry the not-light harp back to Jack's house. When we get to Jack's yard, Jack sets the harp down and heads for the beanstalk. "Let's do this!" he cries.

"Um, Jack, you're forgetting the harp," I say.

"Are you kidding?" he says. "We can't carry it all the way back up! And anyway, I think you guys should hold on to it. Just in case you don't find the goose. That way, you can sell the harp and try to find another goose that lays golden eggs. Maybe they sell them at the market. They're probably really expensive."

"I think there's only one goose that lays golden eggs," Jonah says.

"Yeah. And he belongs to Magnus and Philippa," I add. "We should give the harp back. We're going to find that goose. So I'll feel better if we return the harp."

"If you insist," Jack says with a sigh.

We all grab hold of the harp, and maneuver our way up the beanstalk.

So. Heavy.

Once we have Prince back, all this will have been worth it.

This time the castle door is closed.

I guess the giants learned from their mistakes. They're no fools.

"Let's go around back," Jack suggests. "Maybe there's a basement window we can go through. Or a doggie door."

"I don't think they have a dog," I point out. "We would have noticed it. Especially if it were giant."

"But they have a goose," Jonah says. "Maybe there's a goose-sized door."

"Good point!" I say. "Let's look."

We heave the harp over to the other end of the castle and peer around the side like we did earlier. The garden looks very nice with the pruned rosebushes. Magnus and Philippa are not out here.

Good.

The three of us run into the garden. And there, on the side of the castle, is a small (well, relatively small) door with a flap. Above the flap is a small portrait of a white goose with a pale yellow beak. The word *NELLY* is painted in pink letters above the portrait.

There really is a goose door!

"You called it, Jonah," I say, giving my brother a high five.

"Yay!" he says.

I'm glad that things are going right for Jonah again. He was really down before.

The goose door is pretty much just our size, so we don't even need to crawl through it. The three of us push through the heavy plastic flap and then we're inside the living room again.

I hear Magnus snoring in the bedroom. I hear Philippa humming in the kitchen.

"Okay," I whisper, putting the harp back on its stand. Phew. It feels really good to give it back. "Let's find that goose!"

Jack goes running down the hall and into one of the bedrooms. A minute later, he comes running out with a goose in his arms. Wow, that was quick!

"That must be Nelly!" Jonah says.

She's not as giant as I feared — she's actually my size. And she looks just like the painted portrait on the goose door. Nelly is white and fluffy with a pale yellow beak. And, from the expression on her face, very annoyed.

I gape at Jack. "How'd you find the goose so fast?"

"Because I found her last time," Jack explains. "Nelly was in the room I told you I'd checked. She has a bunch of toys, too. They seem to take good care of her."

Jonah tilts his head. "But, Jack, why'd you lie and say the goose wasn't there yesterday?"

Jack hangs his head for a moment. "Because I want the goose. More than you'll ever know. So I was planning to go back and get her for myself. A goose that lays golden eggs means my mum and I will never want for anything. After being poor for so long. I need this goose. And I'm taking her for myself. Sorry, guys."

Jonah's mouth drops open. He seems totally speechless.

I gasp. "No! Jonah and I have to give the goose to Devin. You know that, Jack!"

Jonah looks so disappointed. "Yeah, what happened to 'A deal is deal'?"

“I’m really sorry. I was hoping you wouldn’t come back up today, and that you’d never know I was taking it.” Jack’s hazel-green eyes look teary. He clutches Nelly firmly in his arms. “But I’m not letting you give the goose to Devin.”

So that’s why he tried to convince us not to come back! He wasn’t worried about Jonah being turned into bread. He wanted the goose for himself. “Hand over the goose!” I demand.

“No!” Jack says, and goes running for the goose door.

“Come back here!” I yell.

“FEE, FI, FO, FUM. I SMELL THE BLOOD OF AN ENGLISHMAN.”

Oh, no.

THUD. THUD-THUD.

“AHHH!” I cry. “Run!”

Jonah and I go racing for the goose door. Jack, with the goose in his arms, is just ahead of us.

“Philly!” comes Magnus’s booming voice. “Those horrible children thieves have Nelly!”

“What?” Philippa cries. “Oh, goodness, they wouldn’t take our dear pet goose!” She starts sobbing.

Oh, crumbs. Double, triple, quadruple crumbs. A hundred million crumbs.

THUD. THUD-THUD. "I see you!" Magnus says.

I turn around very slowly. Looming right behind me is the giant. With a crying Philippa right behind him.

AHHHH!

"RUN AS FAST AS YOU CAN!" I cry, and Jonah, Jack, and I all go rushing through the flap in the goose door again.

We hurry around the side of the castle and straight to the cloud walkway that leads to the beanstalk.

"COME BACK HERE THIS INSTANT!" Magnus shouts at us as the front door opens.

"I'm really sorry!" Jack calls over his shoulder. "But no!"

Jack is trying to get onto the beanstalk, but Nelly the goose is putting up a fight. She's flapping her wings while he's trying to get control of her.

"You'll hurt her!" I cry.

THUD-THUD. THUD-THUD.

We all turn around. Magnus is running toward us! And Philippa is right behind him.

AHHHH.

SQUAWK! Nelly yelps.

I have to get that goose from Jack! I need her.

Jack wants the goose for himself. I want her so I can get Prince back. But Nelly isn't either of OURS. We're both stealing her from her owners.

I hang my head. My stomach churns. But what choice do I have?

I have to get that goose to Devin or we'll never see Prince again. We'll have to return to Smithville without him.

There's no chance of me letting that happen.

I turn again and look at Magnus rushing toward us. Behind him, Philippa is weeping and calling for her dear Nelly.

As the giants are running down the walkway, I see Jack is still having a terrible time trying to get Nelly under his arm.

"Jonah, I have an idea," I whisper. "You tickle Jack. I'll grab the goose."

THUD-THUD. THUD!

"Come back here, you thieves!" Magnus yells as he nears us.

Jonah and I rush up to Jack by the beanstalk. The goose is flapping her wings like crazy, trying to get away from Jack.

"Stay still, Goose!" Jack tells Nelly as nicely as he can. "Please!"

"Now!" I yell at Jonah.

Jonah tickles Jack under his arm.

"Hey, stop that!" Jack says, wiggling around. He is the opposite of laughing.

I grab the goose. "I have her!" I say, and leap onto the beanstalk.

When you've done this five times, it's not that hard even with a goose.

Nelly is flapping her wings and trying to escape, but I have her securely under my arm.

"I can't believe you took her from me!" Jack shouts, jumping onto the beanstalk after me and sliding down. He's not far above me. I hope he doesn't try to steal her back. Especially on the beanstalk!

"I had to!" I say.

I see Jonah leap onto the beanstalk after Jack and start to slide down, too. Phew. At least he escaped the giants.

Nelly tries to flap her wings, but I hold her securely under one arm. I use the other arm to grab on to side stems as I climb down.

Squawk! Squawk-squawk! Nelly protests.

"I'm sorry, Nelly!" I say. "I don't have a choice."

The giants are standing at the edge of the cloud walkway right by the beanstalk, looking down at us. They won't try climbing down the beanstalk, right? It wouldn't support their weight. Would it?

"There's always a choice!" Magnus yells. "We could talk it out!"

Tears sting my eyes. This is the worst! Nelly belongs to the nice giants. Not to me. Not to Devin.

I think about Prince being stuck forever with the trader who went back on his deal — twice!

I have to save my dog. Not just for me, but for Jonah. He loves Prince so much. And so do my parents. I have to get Prince back.

"I'm really sorry!" I call up again to Magnus and Philippa, and climb down the beanstalk as fast as I can. When I'm about three-quarters of the way to the bottom, I see Jack's shabby little wood house and barn. And wait — a man is there, too — standing right beside the beanstalk. A man with curly hair staring upward. It's Devin! And is that Prince sitting behind him? It is!

Devin must have been waiting for us to come down with the goose.

This is perfect. I'll give Devin the goose, and that's it. Jack won't get his hands on Nelly again.

I'm doing this for Prince. To save Prince. I have no choice!

But I'm stealing the giants' beloved pet. I'm no better than Jack. Or Devin.

Just a bit farther and I'll be at the bottom.

"I need that goose!" Jack cries from just above me. "To make sure we'll never go hungry or be cold again!" He reaches down to grab Nelly from me.

"No!" I say. "Stop it!"

"Leave my sister alone!" Jonah yells. He's shimmying down the beanstalk and is a few feet above Jack.

"Ahh!" I hear Jack yelp. "I'm slipping. I can't — "

Jack starts to fall.

I'm the only one who can save him.

But I can't catch him with a goose in my arms.

The only way to save Jack's life is to let the goose go. At least geese can fly, right?

"Jack!" Ada yells, running out of the house to the yard. "Oh, no, my darling son!"

"Ahh!" Jack says as he drops. "I'm falling!"

I suck in a breath and let the goose go so that I can grab Jack's wrist.

Nelly squawks and flies up, up, up.

Jack gasps and is able to grab on to a side stem and get his footing again. He looks at me. "You saved my life."

"Abby!" Jonah says, staring at me in awe. "You're a hero!"

"But I let the goose go," I cry. My eyes are stinging so hard from tears, I can't see. "We'll never get Prince back now."

Jonah's face crumples.

I look up. Nelly is half climbing, half flying back up the beanstalk.

Our only chance of saving Prince is gone.

chapter twelve

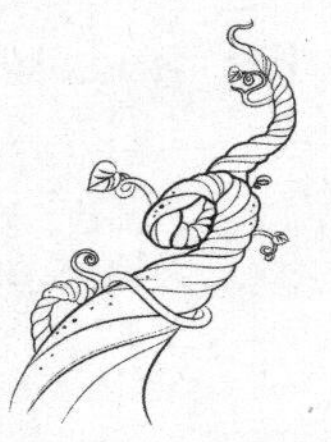

What's Good for the Goose

We slide down the rest of the way, and all jump down to the ground. Ada grabs Jack and pulls him into a hug.

"You fool!" Devin yells at me. "The goose got away!"

I look up. Nelly is almost to the clouds.

"Nelly!" I hear Magnus's voice boom. "Nelly! I'm coming for you."

I can see the giant's huge boots on the beanstalk. The beanstalk starts to shake.

Oh, no! Magnus is coming down? But the goose is going up!

"Don't worry!" Devin says. "I have an ax! I'll chop the beanstalk down and the giant will fall to his death!"

Devin has an ax? What, does he carry around an ax at all times?

"NO!" I say. "You can't. Magnus and Philippa are nice! Don't hurt him!"

Devin swings the ax over his head. "The giant deserves it after what he did to my boy!"

I stare at Devin. "Your boy?" What is he talking about?

"That horrible giant killed my son!" Devin cries. "Magnus deserves to fall to his death!"

Wait a minute. Suddenly, things are starting to make sense.

I put my hands on my hips and glare at Devin. "You set us up from the start. So that we'd take your beans and grow the beanstalk. Then we'd climb up and steal stuff to make the giant come after us. So *you* could chop down the beanstalk with him on it! You wanted to kill Magnus!"

Devin's eyes fill with tears. "It's true," he admits. "It's all true."

"Why didn't you just plant the beans yourself?" I ask. "Why get us to do it?"

Devin looks at the ground and then up at me. "I'm too old to climb a beanstalk. I'm just a widower with a bad back."

"How did your son meet Magnus in the first place?" Jonah asks.

Devin takes a deep breath. "A fairy gave my son, Elden, ten magic beans."

The fairy! No wonder she wasn't in this story. She was in a different story: Elden's.

"Elden used five of the magic beans to grow the beanstalk," Devin said. "He snuck into the giant's castle and tried to steal a bunch of stuff. But instead of having mercy, the giant killed him. All I got was a note."

"A note?" I ask.

Devin nods. "The note said, 'Your son snuck into the castle. Now he is dead.' It was signed 'Magnus the giant.'"

"Oh, Magnus, really!" Philippa scolds from a quarter of the way down the beanstalk. "What kind of note is that?"

"I'm not good at writing letters," Magnus says sheepishly. "And you weren't home, so I had to write the note myself."

"Wait," I call up to him. "What happened that day, Magnus?"

"I smelled the boy in the castle," Magnus explains. "I did want to eat him, but Philippa told me that was wrong years ago and made me promise I'd never hurt a human child. I kept my word."

"Liar!" Devin yells up. "Then how did my Elden die at your hand?"

"Not at my hand," Magnus responds. "The boy was trying to climb into the cabinet to get my gold coins. And he fell from the cabinet to the floor. That's quite a distance for a human boy."

That's true. We know that firsthand.

"I heard the thud," Magnus continues. "I knew he was dead and I felt terrible. So I wrote a note and then buried him myself."

Oh, poor Elden. Poor Magnus.

"What a sad story," Ada says, dabbing under her eyes.

Very.

I turn to the trader. "Devin, you now know what really happened."

Devin sniffles, but he doesn't say anything.

Maybe Devin and Magnus can reach a truce now.

"And, Magnus," I call up, "we're very sorry we stole your gold and tried to steal Nelly. That was wrong."

"Keep the gold," Magnus says. "I have plenty. At least you brought back the harp. And I'm just so grateful that we have Nelly where she belongs."

Squawk! Nelly says.

"Thank you, Magnus," I say. "That's very generous of you."

"Um, Magnus?" Jonah calls up.

"Yes?" the giant says.

"So you don't really turn people's bones into bread?" Jonah asks.

Magnus laughs. "Of course not! That's just an old song my dad used to sing to me before he died."

"My dad died, too," Jack says. "Sorry for your loss."

"And yours, young man," Magnus says. "And yours, Devin," he adds.

We're all silent for a moment.

"Devin?" Magnus asks.

"What?" Devin mutters.

"Since your son used five of the magic beans, and then

Abby, Jonah, and Jack used the other five, there's no more, right?" Magnus asks.

"Well, I do have one more," Devin says. "Abby, Jonah, and Jack only used four. But I don't want anything to do with beanstalks ever again. Here," he says, pulling the bean from his pocket. "I'll throw it up to you so that no one can ever get to your castle without your permission again."

Devin winds his arm like a baseball player and tosses up the bean. I watch it sail higher and higher until it goes through a cloud. Magnus's huge arm darts out from the top of the clouds and his hand snatches up the bean.

"Got it!" Magnus calls. "So maybe you can chop down the beanstalk? Now that you don't have a beef with me anymore?"

"Okay," Devin agrees. "We have a truce. And this time, I really mean it. Let's chop this thing down. You two climb back up to the top first," he tells Magnus and Philippa.

"Hey, Magnus?" Jack calls up. "Can I ask you something? How'd you get so rich anyway?"

"Philly and I stayed in school and then both worked very hard every day until our retirement," Magnus explains. "We squirreled away quite a lot of savings."

"So that's how you bought the goose and the harp?" I ask.

"Actually, we found Nelly as a stray baby goose wandering around the clouds. We put up Lost Gosling ads in other kingdoms, but no one claimed her. She's been with us ever since. Years now. As for the harp, that was a gift from my brother, Morty."

Wow. So Philippa and Magnus really did come by all their wealth honestly. I'm so glad we learned the truth about them.

The beanstalk shakes as Magnus and Philippa make their way back up through the clouds.

"Okay! We're on the cloud walkway," Magnus shouts down to us.

"Bye, Magnus and Philippa," I call up to the giants. "Thanks for understanding!"

"Bye, dear!" Philippa calls back.

Devin picks up the ax. "Elden sure loved chopping wood," he says. "I gave him an ax for his birthday." Tears well in his eyes.

"Aww," Ada says. "There, there, Devin. You take a breather. I'll chop down the beanstalk. I've been chopping wood on my own for years."

Ada takes the ax and gives the beanstalk five good whacks. It comes falling down in the far side of the field with a *THUD*.

"I'll chop it up a little every day," Ada says. "Maybe we can make a pottage out of it."

"Or a fort," Jonah suggests.

Ada smiles. "We'll see."

"Well, Jonah and I had better get home," I say, looking at my watch. I turn to where Devin is standing with Prince. Finally. Prince is ours again! "Come on, Prince. Time to go. It's almost seven a.m. there! And we don't even know how to get home!"

"Where is home?" Jack asks.

"A place called Smithville," Jonah says.

"How do you get there? Another magical beanstalk?" Ada asks.

"No," I say. "But it does involve magic. We need to find a regular object that turns purple and swirls. Let me know if you see anything like that. As soon as possible. The three of us have to get going for real."

Devin steps forward in front of Prince. "Um, sorry, but you can't take Prince. You still owe me something for him."

He has to be kidding. After all this?

"Devin, come on," I say, my annoyance bubbling over.

He lifts his chin. "The giants have their riches and Nelly the goose. Jack has the gold coins. And what do I have?" He hangs his head. "Nothing. Except for sweet, cute Prince." He kneels down and scoops up Prince, petting him and cooing at him.

That is OUR dog!

"We don't have anything to trade you for him," I say. "You saw what happened with the goose."

"Oh, well," Devin responds. "I'm very sorry, but like you guys said, a deal is a deal. Come, Prince, time to go home. TO MY HOUSE."

Devin starts to walk away with Prince in his arms.

Prince looks back at me and Jonah. *Ruff-ruff!* he barks, tilting his head to the left and then to the right.

But Devin keeps walking ahead.

Noooo!

chapter thirteen

The Right Stuff

"Wait!" Jack calls.

Devin turns around.

Jack steps forward. "If you give Prince back to Abby and Jonah, I'll give you all of the gold coins, Devin."

I gasp.

Jonah's mouth drops open.

Devin stares at Jack. "You'd give me all of the gold? Just so they can have their dog back?"

Jack hangs his head. "Yes. Abby saved my life. Even after I tried to steal the goose for myself. So I'm going to do right by her."

I'm too shocked to say a word.

Jack turns to his mother. "Sorry, Mum. We won't be rich, after all. But it's the right thing to do."

"Oh, Jackie," Ada says, pulling him into a hug. "Don't be sorry. I'm so proud of you. You're a hero, too, now."

Jack hugs his mom, then turns to me. "I'm sorry I tried to trick you and Jonah about the goose. You helped me, and I betrayed you. That was wrong — no matter the reason. I'm really sorry."

Huh. Maybe the reason DOES matter, though. Jack tried to steal Nelly to ensure he and his mother would survive. That's a pretty good reason!

Just like Jonah and I had a good reason for stealing the goose from the giants.

Right and wrong. Wrong and right. Which is which? I think about Frankie and Robin and their fight. I guess people can be wrong and right at the same time.

"Thank you so much, Jack," I say. "That's really amazing of you."

He smiles at me, then turns to Jonah. "Want to know something, Jonah?" Jack asks.

Jonah nods. "Yes, I do want to know something."

"Remember when you thought you messed things up for me by telling me about the magic beans in the first place?" Jack asks.

Jonah nods.

"You didn't," Jack says. "I messed things up for myself by getting greedy and selfish. The gold coins were never mine to start with. So don't feel bad about how things turned out in the end, okay?"

Jonah smiles. "That does make me feel a little better." He turns to me. "But not much. Now Jack and his mom are poor again. And it's my fault. We came into his story. If we hadn't, I wouldn't have messed anything up. And Jack would still have his money. Maybe we should stop going into fairy tales."

I gasp. Stop going into stories?

He can't be serious. Can he?

I stare at my brother. He looks VERY serious.

Not go through the mirror anymore? Not meet fairy tale characters?

Not mess up their stories . . .

I bite my lower lip. Maybe Jonah is right.

But I love going into stories.

And now I have a new dilemma, don't I?

"But, Jonah," I say, "if we hadn't come into the story, Magnus wouldn't be alive. We saved him."

Jonah eyes light up. "Oh. Right."

"That's a big deal," Jack says. "You saved someone's life."

"I guess we did," Jonah says.

"Not bad, little soccer star," Jack says.

"I'm not a soccer star," Jonah says with a sigh. "You are."

"You will be. You just need to keep practicing."

Jonah smiles again. "Thanks, Jack."

Devin puts down Prince, then kneels beside him and pets him. "You can go to your rightful family now, Prince. I sure had fun taking care of you the past couple of days."

Ruff! Prince barks. He gives Devin's cheek a lick, then runs over to me and Jonah.

"Yay!" we both say at the same time, dropping down to smother Prince in hugs and kisses.

"I'll get you the gold," Ada says to Devin.

Devin shakes his head. "I changed my mind. I'm so impressed with your sacrifice, Jack. You can keep the gold coins. All of them. I wish you could have met my son. You would have been a good influence on him."

"Awesome!" Jonah exclaims, pumping his fist in the air.

Yes! Jack and his mom get the gold, Jonah and I get Prince, the giant gets to live, and everyone wins. Well, except Devin.

"Devin," Ada says, walking up to him. "I want to thank you. That was very generous of you."

Devin blushes. "You're welcome, Ada."

"Perhaps once we're settled in our new home," Ada says, "you can come over for dinner and pie."

"I'd like that," Devin says, tipping his hat. "I'd like that very much."

Ada smiles.

Jack smiles.

Jonah smiles.

I smile.

I have a feeling that Devin may join Ada and Jack for dinner very soon. Devin is missing a son. And Jack is missing a dad. And you never know when love will strike, right?

"Well, Jonah," I say, "we really do have to go now."

Jonah nods, then turns to Devin. "Mr. Trader?" he asks.

Devin smiles at him. "Yes, Jonah?"

"I bet you could find a stray dog to adopt," Jonah says. "I saw two cute dogs with no collars roaming around the market looking for crumbs the other day."

Devin nods. "I think I'll do just that. In fact, I think I'll adopt both of them. Great idea, Jonah."

"I just love dogs," Ada says with a big smile.

"Now that everything is okay again," Jonah says to me, "I wish I could stay longer and play one more soccer game with Jack."

I glance at my watch, which I'm really happy I didn't have to trade. It's six fifty-five in the morning at home. Oh, no! My parents' alarm has already gone off. We have to be home any minute and we still don't know where the portal is!

"Sorry, Jonah," I say. "But we're out of time. And we need to find the portal."

"I bet it's in the beanstalk," Jonah says.

"But we cut down the beanstalk," I remind him.

"There's still a stump," Jonah says. He hurries over to where the bottom is. "Look! It's purple!"

I run over. He's right. It is purple. Which means it could

be the portal! Or a rotting vegetable. But, hopefully, a portal. We don't have a lot of time to find it.

I knock on it three times. It starts to swirl.

"It's the portal!" I cry. "We have to go!"

Jonah high-fives Jack.

"Good luck!" Jack says to him, and Jonah gives him another hug.

"Bye, Jack," I say.

"Bye, Abby," Jack says.

Then to my surprise he leans forward and gives me a kiss on the cheek.

Ahhh!

My face burns. Did I really have a crush on Jack?

Maybe I did. Maybe I do?

"I hope I see you both again someday," Jack says.

"Me too," I say, still blushing.

Jonah and I wave good-bye to Ada and Devin, who wave back.

Jonah scoops up Prince in his arms. And we jump through the swirling purple portal.

chapter fourteen

Dilemma Time

We land back in the basement of our house in Smithville.

"I'm so happy to have Prince back," I say, giving our wonderful dog a few scratches behind his ears. He loves those. I rub his head, too. "I missed him!"

"Me too," Jonah says. "Nothing felt right without him. He really is part of the family."

Exactly. "I know what you mean."

"I'm so glad everything worked out," Jonah says. "But that was a close one."

I smile. "Sure was."

"I do think I want to keep going into stories after all," Jonah says. "Do you?"

I nod. "Definitely." I look at the mirror. "Maryrose?" I call.

I try knocking to see if the fairy who lives in our mirror will answer. Sometimes she does. Sometimes she doesn't.

The mirror ripples. Yay! We see the outline of Maryrose's face in the mirror and her long hair.

"Hi!" I say. "We just came from *Jack and the Beanstalk*." But of course she already knows that since she's the one who sent us there.

"Hi, Abby and Jonah," she says. "You did a great job."

"I almost decided never to go into stories again," Jonah says. "But then I changed my mind."

Maryrose smiles. "Well, I hope you'll keep it up. You're almost ready for the big one. But making tough decisions isn't easy, is it?"

No, it's not. I think of Frankie and Robin.

I'm about to ask Maryrose another question — what does she mean by the "big one"? — but her face fades until the ripples are gone.

"Come on," I tell Jonah. "We only have a couple minutes to get back to our rooms."

We start up the basement steps with Prince on our heels, and Jonah says quietly, "Abby?"

"Yeah?"

"*Jack and the Beanstalk* is still my favorite story."

"Good," I say. "I'm glad."

"And when Nana used to read it to us," he says, "I used to wish Jack was my big brother. So it was really awesome to meet him."

"I know," I say. I know, I know, I know. The big brother he never had.

"I mean, Jack *was* great," Jonah says. "But I also saw that he wasn't perfect. He did trick us about Nelly the goose. I guess no one is perfect."

"That's true," I say.

"But," Jonah goes on with a sheepish smile, "I don't think I need a big brother. I would never trade you, Abby. I'm glad you're my big sister."

Aww. Me too. My eyes get all teary. Is someone chopping onions in here?

I squeeze him into a hug. Maybe I had to get a little jealous to see how much I like having Jonah for a little brother.

When we reach the top of the stairs, instead of going up to his bedroom, Jonah heads for the living room.

"I'm gonna go practice my side kicks in the yard," Jonah says. "I'm getting really good now! And like Jack said, it's all about practicing."

I love his new confidence. And my parents will definitely be surprised to see him practicing soccer before school. They'll be glad to see Jonah is feeling better and working hard.

"Have fun!" I say with a yawn. Jonah heads off. I hear the sliding glass door to the backyard open and shut and then a foot kicking a ball.

I head upstairs with Prince. In my room, I go over to my jewelry box on my dresser and pick it up. My nana gave the box to me. It's decorated with all the fairy tale characters. But whenever Jonah and I return from a story, the characters change to match how we changed their story.

Before, Jack was standing next to a giant beanstalk with a goose in his arms. Now? He's wearing a suit and standing next to his mom and Devin! And his mom is wearing a wedding dress and Devin is in a tux! And two little puppies are curled at their feet.

Aw! Everything turned out all right.

"Abby!" my dad calls, knocking on my bedroom door. "Time to get up! You'll never believe it. Your brother is practicing soccer outside already!"

"I believe it," I say to myself with a smile before climbing back into bed to pretend I just woke up.

"Hi, Abby," Frankie says when I arrive at school that morning. She's waiting for me in front of my locker.

I open my locker and put my jacket inside, then close it.

"Hi," I say.

"So what do you think I should do?" she asks. "Should I tell Daria I can't go to her party tomorrow because I already have plans?"

Right. The movie night dilemma.

I remember what my mom said. "What do you think you should do?" I ask Frankie.

She tilts her head. "Well, I do already have plans. With you and Robin. But they're the SAME plans every week. And this is a birthday party. It's a once-a-year thing."

"You have to do what feels right to you," I say.

I really think that's the best answer. What feels right to ME might not feel right to Frankie or Robin. And that's okay.

"But Robin's upset," Frankie reminds me. "So I should go to movie night, right?"

I can't answer that for her. That has to be up to Frankie, not me.

"Well, tell me this, then," Frankie says. "Why aren't YOU upset about the idea of me not going to movie night?"

I think about what happened in Tradetown. "I was upset at the beginning. At least a little. I get why you want to go the party. But I also get why Robin is upset. Plans are plans. But sometimes, plans change."

Just like sometimes stories change. And it can save lives when they do!

"I see both sides," I explain. "You're both right."

Frankie nods. "Okay. I know what to do."

"Really?" I ask. "What?"

Robin heads toward us. Her strawberry-blond hair is in a low ponytail. "Frankie, I think I was being a bit harsh," she says. "You should go to Daria's party."

Frankie laughs. "But I already decided to hang out with you guys. Your feelings are more important to me than a party. You're my best friends."

Aww.

Robin grins. "I really appreciate that. And I feel the same way. That's why you should go to the party. But I was thinking — why don't we have our movie night *tonight*? That way we can ALL be there. As long as it works for both of you. I talked to my parents and they said tonight works, too."

"Oh!" I say. "I can do tonight!"

"Me too," Frankie says with a big grin.

"Hurrah!" they both cheer.

"Fantastic!" Penny exclaims, pushing her way between us. "If movie night is tonight, then I can come!"

"Oh," I say. "Yay?"

She flips her hair off her shoulder. "It's perfect. It can be at my house."

"I still get to choose the movie," Robin says quickly.

"If you insist," Penny says. "But I have some suggestions. And I'm picking the snacks."

Sigh. "Sounds fine to me," I say. And it kinda does. Penny has a good couch for curling up on.

"You know," Penny says, "it would make sense to move movie night to Friday night permanently, don't you think? It'll be Penny, Robin, Abby, and Frankie movie night." She grins. "We'll call it PRAFM!"

Oh, beans.

Follow Abby down the yellow brick road . . .

Look for:

Whatever After Special edition #2: **ABBY** in **OZ**

acknowledgments

Giant-sized thank-yous to:

Everyone at Scholastic: Aimee Friedman, Rachel Feld, Taylan Salvati, Olivia Valcarce, Mindy Stockfield, Charisse Meloto, Lauren Donovan, Tracy van Straaten, Robin Hoffman, Melissa Schirmer, Elizabeth Parisi, Abby McAden, David Levithan, Lizette Serrano, Emily Heddleson, Sue Flynn, and everyone in the School Channels and in Sales.

My amazing agents, Laura Dail, Samantha Fabien, Austin Denesuk, and Matthew Snyder, and queen of publicity, Deb Shapiro.

Lauren Walters, Alyssa Stonoha, and Katie Rose Summerfield, who do all the stuff.

Thank you to all my friends, family, writing buddies, and first readers: Targia Alphonse, Tara Altebrando, Bonnie Altro, Elissa Ambrose, Robert Ambrose, Jennifer Barnes, the Bilermans, Jess Braun, Jeremy Cammy, the Dalven-Swidlers, Julia DeVillers, Elizabeth Eulberg, the Finkelstein-Mitchells, Stuart Gibbs, Alan Gratz, the Greens, Adele Griffin, Anne

Heltzel, Farrin Jacobs, Emily Jenkins, Lauren Kisilevsky, Maggie Marr, the Mittlemans, Aviva Mlynowski, Larry Mlynowski, Lauren Myracle, Melissa Senate, Courtney Sheinmel, Jennifer E. Smith, Christina Soontornvat, the Swidlers, Robin Wasserman, Louisa Weiss, Rachel and Terry Winter, the Wolfes, Maryrose Wood, and Sara Zarr.

Extra love to Chloe, Anabelle, and Todd.

And to my Whatever After readers: Thank you for reading my books!

Read all the Whatever After books!

Whatever After #1: FAIREST of ALL

In their first adventure, Abby and Jonah wind up in the story of Snow White. But when they stop Snow from eating the poisoned apple, they realize they've messed up the whole story! Can they fix it — and still find Snow her happy ending?

Whatever After #2: IF the SHOE FITS

This time, Abby and Jonah find themselves in Cinderella's story. When Cinderella breaks her foot, the glass slipper won't fit! With a little bit of magic, quick thinking, and luck, can Abby and her brother save the day?

Whatever After #3: SINK or SWIM

Abby and Jonah are pulled into the tale of the Little Mermaid — a story with an ending that is *not* happy. So Abby and Jonah mess it up on purpose! Can they convince the mermaid to keep her tail before it's too late?

Whatever After #4: DREAM ON

Abby and Jonah are lost in Sleeping Beauty's story, along with Abby's friend Robin. Before they know it, Sleeping Beauty is wide awake and Robin is fast asleep. How will Abby and Jonah make things right?

Whatever After #5: BAD HAIR DAY

When Abby and Jonah fall into Rapunzel's story, they mess everything up by giving Rapunzel a haircut! Can they untangle this fairy tale disaster in time?

Whatever After #6: COLD as ICE

When their dog, Prince, runs through the mirror, Abby and Jonah have no choice but to follow him into the story of the Snow Queen. It's a winter wonderland . . . but the Snow Queen is mean, and she FREEZES Prince! Can Abby and Jonah save their dog . . . and themselves?

Whatever After #7: BEAUTY QUEEN

Abby and Jonah fall into the story of *Beauty and the Beast*. When Jonah is the one taken prisoner instead of Beauty, Abby has to find a way to fix this fairy tale . . . before things get pretty ugly!

Whatever After #8: ONCE upon a FROG

When Abby and Jonah fall into the story of The Frog Prince, they realize the princess is so rude they don't even *want* her help! But will they be able to figure out how to turn the frog back into a prince all by themselves?

Whatever After #9: GENIE in a BOTTLE

The mirror has dropped Abby and Jonah into the story of Aladdin! But when things go wrong with the genie, the siblings have to escape an enchanted cave, learn to fly a magic carpet, and figure out WHAT to wish for . . . so they can help Aladdin and get back home!

Whatever After #10: SUGAR and SPICE

When Abby and Johah fall into *Hansel and Gretel*, they can't wait to see the witch's cake house (yum). But they didn't count on the witch trapping them there! Can they escape and make it back to home sweet home?

Whatever After #11: TWO PEAS in a POD

When Abby lands in *The Princess and the Pea*—and has trouble falling asleep on a giant stack of mattresses—everyone in the kingdom thinks SHE is the princess they've all been waiting for. Though Abby loves the royal treatment, she and Jonah need to find a real princess to rule the kingdom . . . and get back home in time!

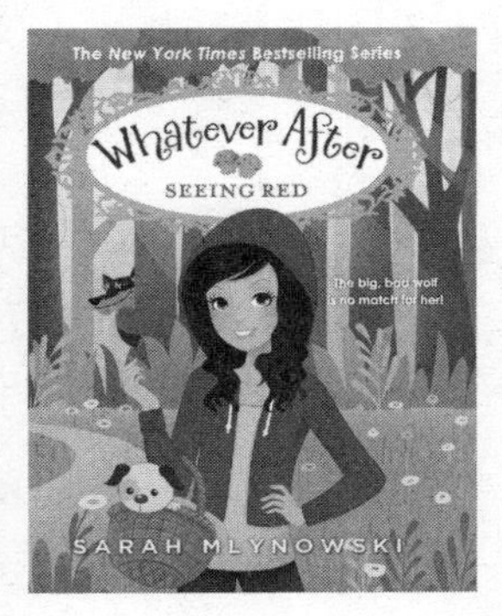

Whatever After #12: SEEING RED

My, what big trouble we're in! When Abby and Jonah fall into *Little Red Riding Hood*, they're determined to save Little Red and her grandma from being eaten by the big, bad wolf. But there's quite a surprise in store when the siblings arrive at Little Red's grandma's house.

Whatever After Special edition #1: ABBY in WONDERLAND

In this Special Edition, Abby and three of her friends fall down a rabbit hole into *Alice's Adventures in Wonderland*! They meet the Mad Hatter, the caterpillar, and Alice herself . . . but only solving a riddle from the Cheshire Cat can help them escape the terrible Queen of Hearts. Includes magical games and an interview with the author!

about the author

Sarah Mlynowski is the *New York Times* bestselling author of the Whatever After series, the Magic in Manhattan series, *Gimme a Call*, and a bunch of other books for teens and tweens, including the Upside-Down Magic series, which she cowrites with Lauren Myracle and Emily Jenkins. Originally from Montreal, Sarah now lives in the kingdom of Manhattan with her very own prince charming and their fairy tale–loving daughters. Visit Sarah online at sarahm.com and find her on Instagram, Facebook, and Twitter at @sarahmlynowski.